Hanger Stout, Awake!

Books by Jack Matthews

FICTION

BITTER KNOWLEDGE
HANGER STOUT, AWAKE
THE TALE OF ASA BEAN
THE CHARISMA CAMPAIGNS
PICTURES OF THE JOURNEY BACK

NON-FICTION

ARCHETYPAL THEMES IN THE MODERN STORY
(Editor)
COLLECTING RARE BOOKS FOR PLEASURE
AND PROFIT

POETRY

AN ALMANAC FOR TWILIGHT

Hanger Stout, Awake!

Jack Matthews

1977
Hock-Hocking Books
Athens, Ohio

Library of Congress Catalog Card Number: 67-19192
Printed in the United States of America

This book is dedicated to the
Hanger Stouts of this world.

Hanger Stout, Awake!

The events in this story take place sometime in the mid-1960's, in a small Ohio town.

Quite a few people have asked me whatever happened to Hanger after the novel's end. This is a question I cannot answer; but whatever has happened, I think Hanger is all right. If he isn't, we're all in a lot of trouble.

Jack Matthews

I

THE FIRST THING I notice was they were driving this Caddy and it was a new one. The big man stood and watch me while I took the flat tire off. He was half a head taller than me and he had sort of blond hair in the back of his head and he was bald in front. He took off his sunglasses and watch me change the tire and I could see two little dents in his nose where the glasses fit. His eyes were real light color.

The other one was over at the cigarette machine, juggling the knob, and he was kind of little. Not as big as me. He wore regular reading glasses with them sunglasses that clip over them. He looked a little bit like a teacher.

The big one kept watching me close while I am changing the tire. But at first I didn't pay no attention because I was still thinking of Penny, who was away to summer camp, where she was a counselor, and she hadn't written any letters to me. She had just finished her first year at college, where she is getting all A's, practically, and naturally I didn't go to college because I barely made it through high school and didn't want to go anyway. But Penny and me had been drifting apart ever since high school. It wasn't my idea, I can tell you that. She thought I wasn't good enough for her because I was working in a filling station and she was going to college.

Pretty soon, the big one starts to talk to me and I can't think about Penny no more.

Right before this, I had just bang my knuckle against the tire rack when my hand slipped. It sliced a little of the skin away there, but I have bang and cut my knuckles up so much I do not ever notice little things like that.

But this man noticed it. He said, Didn't that hurt?

I told him it didn't. I didn't even notice such things.

Let me see your hands, he said.

So I stood up and let him look at all the scars on them, plus a few fresh cuts I always got.

You say you don't notice things like that? he said.

Not so you would notice, I said.

He shook his head sideways once or twice like that made him pause to think. He said, You must have a high threshold of pain, my friend.

I told him I didn't know about that. And then I got back to work on the tire. I am the sort of person that would rather work than talk, any old day.

You handle tire-changing tools real good, he says.

Yes, I said.

I started pounding the hubcap into place with my hand like I always do, and this man leans over and says, You did that fast. How old are you?

I am eighteen, I told him.

And how much do you weigh, may I ask?

I told him about a 130. Maybe 135.

Very lean, he says, sounding pleased. Very lean. And you're about five ten, I would say?

I guess so.

About five ten, he says again, like he was really thinking of something else while he was saying it, and awful happy about it, whatever it was.

Are you married, may I ask? he said.

I told him no and then squinted right at his face, which I don't do very often. I don't think I ever really once stared in the face of Penny's father even though Penny and I went together about a year.

You probably want to know why I'm so curious, the big man asked. Well I tell you. How about coming over to that Dairy Freeze across the street and I will buy you a milk shake or whatever you want and I'll tell you.

I figure this was just his way of giving me a tip, so I wipe my hands off on the grease rag and the two of us wait for a semi-outfit to go by, then we cross over the street and the little guy is about ten feet behind following us.

This here's Leo Herbert, the big man says, and my name's Dan Comisky.

When he first said that I thought he said something like Come-insky and it wasn't until I got to know him better that I asked him, That's some kind of foreign name, isn't it? and he said, No, it's Irish. Irish as Paddy's pig. People frequently think it's foreign, but it's Irish.

Anyway when we was walking up to the Dairy Freeze window, I saw Phyllis standing there, all eyes because I was walking up to the window with two rich guys she had seen driving up to the filling station in a Cadillac.

What's yours today, Clyde? she asked, looking more at the other two men than at me.

Is that your name? Mr. Comisky said, turning to me and smiling so I could see some gold teeth.

Yes, I said.

The treat's on me, he said to Phyllis. A strawberry milk shake and a Coke for Mr. Herbert and me, and Clyde, he said, turning around slow like he was a big stiff door, you just have anything you like.

I'll have a milk shake, I said to Phyllis, even though she knows what I have.

What's your last name, Clyde? Mr. Comisky said.

I got set for a laugh, because sometimes people laugh when I say Clyde Stout, since I am on the thin side.

But Mr. Comisky and Mr. Herbert just nodded seriously when I say this, like they had already figure I would have a name like that, so the three of us go over to the bench on the shady side of the Freeze and sit down. I know Phyllis is breaking her neck watching us, since she has known my mother for years and she don't miss a thing. I figure she knows the license plate of every car that goes past, she is so nosy. Phyllis is about thirty-five and her husband has had two or three nervous breakdowns, and she supports him.

Clyde, Mr. Comisky says after he's drained half his strawberry milk shake with one drag, I'd like to talk with you. Do you ever gamble, Clyde?

I thought that one over, and I said, Yes I am always in a football pool, and sometimes I go to Millford and bet on the trotters.

Swell, Mr. Comisky said. That's just swell. Millford's where I live.

All this time, Mr. Herbert is just sitting there with his legs crossed in front of him, drinking his Coke without saying nothing and watching the cars go by. I saw Pete, over at the station, get in the Caddy and drive it away from the pump to make room for more cars.

I start in drinking my milk shake so I could get back to work fast. And then I thought of Penny and wondered what she was doing now.

You like this town, Clyde? Mr. Comisky said.

I don't know how to answer a question like that, so I just said it was okay.

Let me tell you about my business, Clyde, Mr. Comisky said. I'm a gambler.

Is that right? I ask.

Sure that's right. I gamble for a living and I make a lot of money on it.

What do you bet on? I said.

Well, lots of things. I bet on cards and horses a lot of the time. And then I like to bet on sporting events. You know, like football games and things like that.

Mr. Herbert hit the bottom of his Coke and the straw made a noise. I notice that Mr. Comisky was through a long time ago so I finish up my milk shake and we all throw the cups in the trash barrel. When we walk back to the station I wave to Phyllis, who was just dying out of curiosity, I could tell.

I was trying to figure out why they was talking to me so much. Mr. Comisky paid Pete for me fixing the flat tire. The tire bell rang and I went out to fill the tank of a '63 Corvair. Its hood had waves on it, it was so hot. When I come back, Mr. Comisky was talking to Pete and then they both stop talking and look at me. Pete was kind of grinning and he nodded his head.

Mr. Comisky come up to me then and said, Clyde, I tell you what.

What? I said.

I'll give you a five-dollar bill if you can hang by your

hands from the runner on that grease rack for two minutes.

I look up at the grease rack and see a '62 Fairlane up there. It was waiting for a lube and oil change.

That's right, Mr. Comisky said. Your boss said he don't mind. So if you want to make five easy bucks, it's yours. You can't touch your feet or nothing. You got to hang free, with your arms straight. No shoulder shrugging or regripping. No pulling yourself up. Most men can't hang over thirty or forty seconds in a position like that. Believe it or not. But if you can hang on for two minutes, I'll give you a five.

Go ahead, Pete said, and he was grinning so hard I knew he couldn't wait to tell everybody I done it. Pete has got a bad natured wife and he gets in all the kidding he can down here at work. He works about seventy or eighty hours a week. That's what happens when you're in business for yourself, he told me.

Well, they wanted me to and I made sure it wasn't a bet because I didn't know how long I could hang from that rack. Pete says, Go ahead. I'll lower the rack and then raise it up and you won't even have to jump for it. If that's okay with you, sir, he says, checking with Mr. Comisky.

Mr. Comisky said sure, so Pete lowered the rack and I put my hands around the rim and then I hear the hydraulic lift make a whirring sound and feel my arms pull up and there I am hanging right up in the air, my feet off the cement a couple feet.

A little while later, Mr. Comisky says, Thirty seconds, and right about then I feel like my arms are about to come out of their sockets. It don't sound like much, but just hanging there like that gets tiring very fast.

I was about to quit when Mr. Comisky says, Forty-five seconds. Then Bo Thompson comes in and says, Clyde, what in the hell you doin up there? Man, you lost your cotton pickin mind?

Pete explains everything to him, and I can tell he's grinning so hard he can hardly talk. I wish his wife was a nicer temper woman. It would make things a lot easier on us down here at the station sometimes.

Anyway, Bo Thompson is just another attendant. I could hear him chewing and snapping away at his Spearmint gum while Pete explained why I was hanging from the grease rack. Then I smelled cigar smoke. I guess it was Mr. Comisky who had lit up.

Things got a little better, maybe, right about then. I mean, my arms got numb. Another half-minute, I was thinking, and I won't be able to let go even if I want to because my hands will be curved around that rack like two pieces of hammered iron.

Then things got kind of dreamy. I was hurting all the way down my sides and all I could think about was Penny and why she hadn't written me a letter and if this was the actual end between her and me. I closed my eyes and saw her face when I did. My arms felt like they was being stretched way out like you see some kid stretch bubble gum out of his mouth. That's the way my arms felt.

Then Mr. Comisky said, Let him down. He done it.

He sounded happy, like he was glad he lost five bucks in two minutes. Some gambler, I thought.

I felt my body sway a little and then my feet was slapped against the cement and I pried my two hands off of that rim and turned around.

By God, Mr. Comisky said. By God.

He give me the five bucks right there and I almost couldn't hold on to the bill, but I did.

He's a natural, Mr. Herbert said, flicking the ash off his cigarette. I hadn't seen Mr. Herbert smile and he didn't smile now. But Mr. Comisky was smiling.

You know, Mr. Comisky said, I had a hunch he could do it. He was saying this to Pete, who was about to split his face grinning.

How was that? Pete ask him.

Why, I saw him cut a big gash out of his knuckle when he was changing my tire. Remember, Leo? He said this to Mr. Herbert, who nodded his head with his eyes closed.

I told Leo here, that boy has it. Strong hands and a high threshold of pain.

Is that what it takes? Pete asked, looking interested, even though he didn't know no more about what this Mr. Comisky was talking about than me.

That's right, Mr. Comisky said, getting real serious. The thing that brings most men down off that bar they're hanging from isn't a loss of strength. No sir. You know what it is?

Pete shook his head.

It's pain, Mr. Comisky said. It's the pain they get in their shoulders. Because the shoulder wasn't meant to stand up under the strain of that constant kind of pulling. Not only that, the blood goes out of the arms. Also the head after awhile, and I've seen boys have hallucinations when they are free hanging from a bar. Yes sir.

Did you have any hallucinations, Clyde? Pete ask me.

I shook my head no, and Bo Thompson, who just come in from filling a '63 Dart with regular, said, How could you tell with Clyde there?

And everyone laughed at that. Even Mr. Comisky, who patted me on the shoulder while he was laughing.

Well, he said, some people can take it. And Clyde here looks to me like he's a natural.

He turn around to me once more and shook my hand. Yes sir, Clyde, he said, I will be getting in touch with you. Meanwhile, let me give you some friendly advice. Okay?

Okay, I said.

Hang every chance you get, he told me.

2

WELL, I didn't know what he was talking about and I didn't think nothing about what he had said. What I did was take that five bucks and get in my '56 Chevy (which I rebuilt a transmission for and put it in last winter) and go downtown. It was about ten-thirty and a slow night, so Pete got tired of kidding me about hanging from the grease rack and he said, Hanger, you go ahead and take off, because I know that five dollars is burning a hole in your pants.

First thing I thought of was I would buy gas with it because my old Chevy isn't very good on mileage, but then I got this other idea, so I drove up to Hillary's Drug Store, which is the only one stays open in this town after nine o'clock. You get sick after nine o'clock in this town and you either go to Hillary's or else you die or wait til eight the next morning.

Anyway, I go into this store and it smells like face powder and things like that. And it's empty because they are about to close up at eleven o'clock. After eleven o'clock in our town, it's every man for himself, sick or not.

I saw this woman who's about forty or fifty and her first name is Annabelle. I don't know her last name and she's always got this kind of make-up on that looks like dried sassafras tea, and she wears great big earrings.

She says hello, Clyde, and I say hello. I can tell the way she talks she's tired and bored.

I ask her if she hasn't got any customers, and she says no, she hasn't.

Then I told her I was looking for a gift for a young lady.

How much do you want to spend? she says.

Oh, about five dollars, I said.

What does your young lady like? Annabelle said.

She likes to read a lot, I said.

Well, Annabelle said, this isn't a bookstore. And then she laughed, and I did too.

Would you like perfume? she ask me, and I said I didn't think so.

How about a nice make-up kit. Here's a nice one selling for $4.95.

I ask her to let me see it and she pulled it out of the glass case and said a bunch of things but I wasn't listening. I didn't think Penny would like it.

Maybe I look around some more, Annabelle, I said.

And she said that was all right with her, so I went outside. Some big hairy bug landed right on my arm, and I jumped. Then some crazy guy come roaring through the square, doing about sixty in a '53 Mercury with twin carbs.

And I went home to bed.

3

WE JUST got one bookstore in our town and it is in the back of a gift store where they have little cuckoo clocks and ashtrays and cups and things like that. There was a little fat man there, smoking a cigarette in a cigarette holder when I come in the next morning. I don't know his name, but I seen him around a lot.

May I help you? he asks.

I would like to buy a book, I told him.

Fine. What book would you like?

I would like to look around first and then pick one out, I said.

He said that would be fine too, so I started looking over the books he had in the shelves. First, there was a lot of cooking books, and then there was some books on mending furniture and buying a house and one book of poetry by Edgar A. Guest.

She likes to read, I said when I noticed the man was looking at me.

I see, he said. It's for a young lady then.

Yes sir, I said.

And she likes literature?

Yes, she does, I said.

Well, then, the man said, let me suggest a nice book of poetry.

I thought he was going to get the book by Edgar A. Guest, because I seen that was poetry, but instead he reach around and got a lot thicker book, called *Singing on the Wings of Time,* by a man named Farad Karaji.

The little fat man held the book and just stared at it with his eyes almost closed, and then he laid his cigarette down with the holder part on the counter. It was right next to a little ashtray shaped like a Mexican hat, and I wonder why he didn't put it in the ashtray.

Then he shook his head sideways in little jerks and said, Beautiful. A beautiful, beautiful book.

How much is it? I ask him.

This book is $4.50. So I buy it and walk out of the store, where it has really gotten hot for so early in the day.

4

RIGHT THEN it is time for me to go to work because it is Saturday and Pete ask me to come in early because we really get busy. That tire bell rings like the bell on a drunken cow. That's what Pete says when we are really busy.

Along about noon, Pete comes to me when I'm checking the spark plugs on a '61 Buick Special, and says, Hanger (because that is what he has called me since Mr. Comisky came by), Hanger, someone wants to talk to you on the phone.

It is my mother and she says, Clyde, the mailman brought you a letter.

Where's it from? I ask her.

It says here, she says, sounding like she hasn't looked at the return address before, but I know better, it says here, P. Barker, Sioux Lodge, Camp Wildwood.

Why, Clyde, Mother said. It must be from Penny.

I told her it probably was since she was the only P. Barker I would know at Camp Wildwood. But Mother never pays attention to sarcasm like that.

Should I open it? she asks. But I told her no, it was my letter, and most likely personal. At least I hope so.

But as it turned out, that letter could of been read at

City Hall, or in the football stadium at half time on Friday night. Because here is the letter which I read all by myself in my bedroom that night.

Dear Clyde,

Judy Wechsler got a letter from Jim Boynton, who said he had seen you last week and you had complained to him about not receiving a letter from me. You can imagine the extent of my surprise when I heard of this. Can you have forgotten the discussion we had after we saw the movie "Thunderball," shortly before I came to Wildwood?

It seems to me that everything was perfectly clear after that discussion, Clyde. It seems to me that I conveyed to you quite clearly that, while I value your friendship *very* highly, and always want to keep you as a friend, a more serious, deeper relationship between us is out of the question.

We have been wonderful high-school friends, Clyde, and let's keep it at that. Doesn't that sound more sensible to you, when you think of it that way?

I hope you will understand now, and refrain from discussing the matter, especially with such people as Jim Boynton, who hardly has an idea of what a secret, or personal confidence, is.

Your friend (always?),
Penny

I read the letter three or four times, and then I turned out the lights and went to bed. I kept thinking about that discussion we had after we saw the movie, and I wonder what she had said that sounded like this letter.

I remember Penny saying something about us being friends always, but I thought that was her way of saying she really liked me. Because why else would you want to always be somebody's friend?

It was beyond me and I couldn't go to sleep. So finally I got up and put on the light and open that book I had bought for Penny. I read the title, *Singing on the Wings of Time*. And then I look at the man's name who wrote it and his picture on the back. He had one of those Arab things over his head and a mustache.

I opened the book to a section called Sayings, and read one of them as follows,

> They told me I was alone,
> Alone in a whirling world
> Of chance,
> Of mystery,
> Of servitude and death,
> But that was ere
> I saw Thee.

I read it out loud two or three times. Then I turn to a section which said, Farad Karaji Recommends, and there was a picture of him, or some other man, sitting on a horse and holding his hand over his eyes. One of the things he recommended said,

> Never let a day pass but what you record
> some portion of that day on paper. Never live
> without keeping a diary or journal. No matter
> how dull your daily life seems to you, there is that part
> of it upon which the mind may seize, illumining it
> until you will be astonished at the depth you possess,

and exalted by the poetry you find dwelling,
humble and unannounced, in your soul.

I also read that over once or twice and thought about it. It sounded a lot like Miss Temple in English class, because she was always saying that people should keep a diary. And if you write a little every day, you would learn to write better.

Penny told me one time that she thought the sun rose and set on Miss Temple.

Before I went to sleep that night, I thought a lot about Farad Karaji's recommendation, and I decided to keep a diary like he said. And that is why I am writing this, only a lot of it was done at the end of each day. That is one reason why I am so sure of how things happened, because I wrote it down every night before I went to bed.

5

I HAD BEEN wanting to get a rear-vision mirror for my '56 Chevy, which I painted all black last fall with some lacquer paint I got special from Bert Wilson's secondhand store.

This new T Bird come in, and I see Bo Thompson start to drop his Coke, because he likes to take care of the expensive new cars. But I beat him to this T Bird and I hear Pete laughing at us because he thinks it's funny the way we fight to get up next to a new car especially if it is a real good one.

Not only that, Pete has been awful jovial and good nature since that day Mr. Comisky come by. He never miss a chance to call me Hanger and things like that, and he told everybody in town about that day. He seem to think it was all my fault, but I remind him he talked me in to it. And I said I would hang again for five dollars, wouldn't he? But when I say that, he knows he has got my goat and he and Bo Thompson just laugh like natural fools. But I tell them I figure they would both hang for five dollars.

I notice Pete don't ever laugh at Mr. Comisky. But it was him that started the whole thing. And I tell him so. Mr. Comisky paid the five dollars to see me hang for two minutes. But Pete just goes ahead and laugh, shaking his head back and forth like he can't get over it. And I tell him the only reason he doesn't laugh at Mr. Comisky is because he's got a new Caddy instead of a '56 Chevy, and he's rich. Pete isn't the sort of person who laughs at a rich person. But this doesn't bother him neither because he just keeps on laughing. I sure wish he didn't have such a mean tempered wife. You should see her or hear her on the telephone.

Anyway, I come back from filling this T Bird with super and Pete says, Hanger, when you going to get that side mirror for your car like you been talking about for so long?

Oh one of these days, I said.

I'll give you twenty percent discount, Pete says. Like on everything else.

Well, thanks, Pete, but I figured I would go out to Rigolo's and get one, I told him.

I should explain that Rigolo's is a junk yard and I figured he would let me have one for a quarter or maybe fifty cents if I went in and got it myself, which I usually do.

That's not a bad idea, Hanger, Pete says. If I was you, I wouldn't invest money on a new mirror for a car as old as yours.

I didn't figure he had to say something like that, and I could see he saw I didn't like it. Maybe Pete felt bad about that crack, because he says, Why don't you take the afternoon off, Hanger, and go get that mirror you been wanting?

I just chew my gum a little bit and look far away, like I'm only half interested in what Pete would say. I didn't like that crack about my Chevy and he saw it.

Everything was quiet for a minute, and then Pete said, Go ahead, Clyde. You deserve some time off.

Well, that did it. He called me Clyde instead of Hanger, so I spit out my gum in the plastic green wastebasket beside the cash register and said, Maybe I will.

Sure, Bo said. You ought to get that mirror for your Chevy, Clyde.

Bo saw it too. I mean, you don't criticize a guy's car. Not if you know how much work and sweat and thinking he's put into it.

6

WELL, that made me feel good. Pete was a pretty good guy sometimes. I went over to the Dairy Freeze and ordered a milk shake and a foot-long coney, and Phyllis asked me all about the two gentlemen she had seen me with last week. I remembered then that I had stayed away from Phyllis ever since Mr. Comisky had paid us a visit because I knew she would be trying to pry everything out of me. Sometimes I figured she might spy for my mother, who was always complaining that she never knew what I was doing. Sometimes Mother would call the filling station, and when she had called the day before just kind of snooping around and wanting to know what I was doing, Pete said I should of told her, Oh just hanging around. And then he laughed like he was going to have a stroke. Which I wish he had.

Anyway today I was having no worry and when Phyllis ask me questions I just answered them like I couldn't care less. It kind of made her short tempered because she likes to feel she's putting things over on people and learning things from them they don't even know themself.

Finally I went to the side of the Dairy Freeze and sat in the shade where Mr. Comisky and Mr. Herbert and me had set that day. For a minute I thought about Mr. Comisky and the five dollars and then I thought about Penny and what she was doing now. That almost spoil my afternoon because I couldn't figure out what we had said after the movie "Thunderball" which made everything clear. I could not figure out what the understanding between us was.

I thought of that poem and was surprise to have all the words in it come back in my mind.

> They told me I was alone,
> Alone in a whirling world
> Of chance,
> Of mystery,
> Of servitude and death,
> But that was ere
> I saw Thee.

I finished the milk shake and coney and got in my Chevy. I waved at Bo as I turned out into the street and then waited as some old man in a tan '65 Fairlane up ahead turned into the automatic laundry owned by Bruce Myers, who has a false eye from the war.

Then I was out in the open, so I glide along about fifty listening to that third cylinder which I figure is due to give trouble before long so that I am using heavy weight oil for a while. But it sound all right.

Then I turn past the airport and the drive-in movie, where Paul Pontius got drunk last Saturday night and had to open the door and vomit right there at the intermission.

And up over the hill and around the curve to Rigolo's junk yard. A lot of people talk about junk yards like they was something ugly but not to me. To me they are beautiful. I get a kind of hiccup in my throat when I drive up to Rigolo's. Especially on a sunny day when you can see the different colors of the metal. The colors have all gone soft and sort of dim from being out in the sun and rain. One reason I come out to Rigolo's alone is I like it quiet. Not only that, you never know what you're going to find that Rigolo will give you or sell to you for a quarter or half a dollar. Like the time I got a magneto off of an old model T, and Rigolo just give it to me. I took it home, only my mother makes me keep it in the shed behind the garage. I would have like to keep it in my bedroom, which sounds sort of crazy to most people, I suppose, but it is the truth. It is a nice looking thing, that magneto.

Rigolo is sitting there at his old desk he use. He look up and sees me and nods. He's a man about fifty with stomach trouble. Every time I go up to him his breath smells like milk of magnesia tablets. He is bald all over and got black eyes, like somebody hit him there, in both eyes, only they are that way all the time. And real white skin.

Hi there, Clyde, Rigolo says and I said hi.

What can I do for you?

I thought I would drop by for that side mirror, I says.

You still looking for a side mirror?

Sure.

He said, I thought you would have got one of them a long time ago. Hell, I'll let you have one for a half-dollar.

I know, I told him. It isn't the money. I want to get one that's just right. I want it to be a nice one, without bubbles in the chrome.

That kind might cost you seventy-five cents, Rigolo said.

That's all right, I told him. I want it to be the right kind.

Well, go out and help yourself, Rigolo says. There is one out there waiting for you if you can only find it.

Rigolo has a way of saying things that really make me listen sometimes. Like then. There is one out there waiting for you if you can only find it. Just the way he says it, like everything in life is this way, and if you want to go out and get it you can.

I went outside and through the gate. It was so hot I could smell all that junk metal and the rust and all the sourness from the upholstery. Sometimes the upholstery swells up from rain and puffs like pillows and busts out and it has got a real funny smell. Kind of like Rigolo's lot is a big attic without a roof or walls, except the hills that are on three sides.

I walk up the first lane of cars and I don't see nothing that would look good on my Chevy. But I did see a couple of hood ornaments that would look good when I have time to think about that. And a real old Hudson with spoke wheels that I always notice there, and like I always do I wonder if I could fix them spoke wheels on my Chevy. But I figure the fittings aren't the same. Still, I could check someday when I have time. Now one of the wheels has a spider web over the spokes, and a grasshopper right there on the fender, where it jumps off and lands on my pant leg. The grass is thick all around the car and smells warm and sour.

And then when I am looking for my rear-vision mirror, I start thinking of Penny again and wondering about her. I remember that she did not like cars the way I do. At least she said she didn't and she didn't want me to talk about them. Every time I would tell her something about my Chevy or what Bo was doing with his '58 Ford, she would take a quick breath like somebody just poured a glass of ice water down her back.

But I saw her one day in an MG with her older sister's fiancé. It was either a '63 or '64, I couldn't get a good enough look, because I was watching Penny. She had her head back and was laughing as they turn the corner. All three of them in the car. I was parked in my Chevy waiting for my mother, who had gone into Schmidt's Grocery for lunch and potato chips, because her '62 Ford was having fender work done on it, where she backed into a fireplug. So they didn't see me, Penny and Charlotte (who is her sister) and her boy friend, who goes to the same college Penny goes to. He majors in history, I think. And his father is a real estate man near Millford. Maybe he knows Mr. Comisky, I thought.

Later on, Penny told me about the MG, and I said, I thought you didn't like cars.

And she said, Oh sometimes I do. And then she just stayed silent, like she didn't want to tell me any more. So I figured she liked them if they were new and expensive. But what did Charlotte's boy friend know about that MG of his? I bet I could tear the engine down and put it back together again, and he probably don't even know where the generator is.

But I shouldn't get mad at him. I should be mad at myself because I should have know right then that Penny didn't like me the way I thought.

Anyway, I thought all about Penny when I was up there in Rigolo's lot, and I walked past six or seven cars, not even noticing if they had side-vision mirrors, I was thinking so hard about her. And that letter she wrote to me.

After a while I come across this '53 Pontiac that has been sideswiped and there is a side mirror on it, right on the side that has been wrecked, only it don't seem to be damage at all. I turned it around where it was hanging from the door. It turned just like a knob from the screws inside the door being smashed from the wreck. It looked okay, and I turn it around about fifty times, seeing what it is like. In fact it was a nice looking mirror, as big as my hand, which Mr. Comisky said was very big for my size and that is one reason why I could hang so long.

But I didn't hurry anything. In fact I stood there about five minutes looking at that mirror before I decide it wasn't just what I wanted. It didn't have no chrome bubbles in it and it was the biggest mirror I ever seen. But I didn't want to have no trouble with the attachment. I saw I would have to drill four holes in my Chevy, and if the mirror didn't fit right, I would have them extra holes there. Which I would have to plug. It was probably too big for my Chevy anyway.

Of course I could have taken it off right there, since I had brung my screwdriver and pliers with me. I don't know why I didn't. But part of it was I got to thinking about Penny again, and nothing seem right. Somehow she was all mixed up with the mirror.

So I didn't get it. I just wave good-by to Rigolo, and drove away. All the way home, I wonder why I didn't get that mirror on the Pontiac. It was probably a custom made job. Rigolo might have charge me a dollar for it, but it was the kind of mirror you don't see every day.

Also while I was driving home I decide to write a letter to Penny. Which I did that night before I went to bed. Also I wrote in my diary.

7

THE NEXT DAY I felt a whole lot better and went back to Rigolo's and got that mirror off the Pontiac for only a dollar. It worked okay.

That afternoon Dad got in. He's a cross-country truck driver for J. T. Oakes. Sometimes he gets home on weekends and sometimes he is gone for four or five weeks at a time. He use to drive for Consolidated and then he was home most of the time, but he isn't any more.

When Dad saw me come in for dinner, he said, There's that old cuss. He always calls me that. How about a drink? he says. And I said that was all right, so Dad got out a couple of root beers from the freezer where they get so cold they hurt your teeth. Dad is the only one does that. The rest of us don't think of it. You know Dad is home because there is always root beer and 7-Up and Pepsi-Cola in the freezer. Sometimes the bottles freeze and bust open and then Mother goes into all kinds of fits. But mostly the kids drink them up almost before they can get cold.

Dad never drinks liquor. He says that is something a truck driver cannot afford to do and if you seen some of the wrecks I have seen you would agree. I drive the station wrecker sometimes, and usually we have a wrecked car over on the gravel beside our lot. Phyllis says it makes her sick to see them, and she must be sick most of the time because the Dairy Freeze is right there across the road and we almost always got one on the gravel. A wrecked car, I mean.

Well, Dad says to me when we are setting out in back in the lawn chairs, Mother tells me you are now pulling your own load.

I guess so, I said.

I think that's fine, Dad says. As a matter of fact it is more than I was doing when I was eighteen. I wasn't pulling my own load until I was twenty. Of course, that was during the depression and they was a difference then. I mean I worked, but I wasn't really pulling my own load.

You can't expect a man to work, I said, unless there is work to do.

That's right, Dad said. That's right. And yet, if you are smart you can sometimes find work to do even when it isn't there.

How can you find it if it isn't there? I ask him.

Well, I don't mean it isn't *really* there. I mean, so far as most people can *see,* it isn't really there. It just takes a smart man to find it.

I see what you mean, I told him.

I knew you would, he said.

And I believe he did. Sometimes it is hard for me to talk with Dad because he understands me.

Did you have a good trip? I ask.

He pulls the root beer bottle out of his mouth with a big pop and says, It was a real good trip. I hit a lot of road repairs west of Kansas City so I took Route 63 to the north. I figure I didn't lose over an hour and a half from my regular time. And from what I heard, I probably saved a half-hour or so from the time I would have made if I had stayed on 27.

Let me see, I said. Sixty-three. Is that the one that goes into Omaha?

Oh no, Dad said. Let me get the map and I'll show you.

I was always crazy about maps and even though I never been to Kansas City or Omaha, I know most of the roads because Dad has gone over them with me ever since I was a boy.

So we sat there and drank our root beers and went over the map until Mother said the hamburgers were on. Then we ate dinner and Carol, my younger sister, play a few records while Dad smoked a cigar and talked with Mother.

One thing he talked about was my older sister, Judith, who is in a nursing home. I haven't seen her for maybe two years now. She has this brain disease that nobody can figure out what it is. The last time I got in a fight was when some boy by the name of Dan Fellows made a crack about my sister Judith and how it must be in the blood. That was when I flunked English in high school. Last year, as a matter of fact, but I didn't need it to graduate. I took it because I thought Penny would be in the class, which she was.

I got in a fight with him then because I am not that dumb. Besides, Carol, my younger sister, is always on the honor roll. I don't know who won the fight because the principal of the school stop it.

The next day Dad drove off for Chicago and St. Paul. And then maybe Seattle, if Oakes got a certain contract they thought they would get. I went to work, and Pete had a headache, so he didn't call me Hanger very often, although he did whenever he talked to me. It was just that he didn't talk to me very often. As a matter of fact, he called me Hanger all the time now, and so did Bo Thompson. I was getting kind of use to it.

There was a wreck right after lunch on Route 123, a state route north of town. It was right beyond Earl Vanscoy's farm, where he raises Brown Swiss cattle. The call came through, and Pete was working on a transmission he didn't want to let go of, so he ask me to take the call.

There wasn't nobody hurt very bad, which was lucky because the car had left the road right behind an abutment and gone into a ditch, hitting a couple of little trees. It was some woman from Pennsville driving and they took her to the hospital but the highway patrolman said she was conscious and just had cuts and bruises, it look like.

It was a blue '64 Plymouth. A nice looking car with a stick shift, which you don't often see a woman driving. I decided to pull the car out backwards. The highway patrolman stood up there directing traffic past. His car was parked in the berm with the red light flashing on top.

Then, when I was just working the log chain under the axle, Jim Boynton pulled up in his '59 Dodge, and yelled out, Hey Hanger, what you doin boy?

I turned around and glared at him, but he kept on with that Hanger business until I climbed out from under the wrecked Plymouth and said, This ain't a good day for Chrysler products, Boynton. You better watch your step.

I figure that would put him down, but the three or four other boys standing there didn't seem to hear. And the highway patrolman was waving a station wagon full of girls past, so he didn't hear neither.

Jim didn't call me Hanger when the girls were near. I figure he didn't notice them. He was too busy watching me with the wrecker.

I pushed a couple of ten- or eleven-year-old farm kids out of the way and nodded at the highway patrolman, who got the signal and waved everybody back. I jerked the hydraulic on and felt my front wheels wobble and go up in the air a little as I lifted the Plymouth. I was on a bad angle, but our old wrecker, which is a '62 Ford, is heavy duty and can lift just about anything.

I got out and let the door swing open while I went back to see if the front wheels would drag. Then I decided to tie the steering wheel of the Plymouth so they would stay straight. The patrolman ask me what was the delay and I told him this was a tough angle to pull the Plymouth out from.

Well, hurry it up if you can, he told me, and I said all right.

I got back in the cab of the wrecker and threw it in drag gear. I edged it forward and got a glance of Jim Boynton standing there with his mouth hanging open, he was so interested in what I was doing. I wish Penny could of seen me like that right then.

The Plymouth came out of the ditch like a soft tooth out of an old dog's mouth, and I dropped it gentle right there at the side of the road. Then I went back and look again and decided since the steering wheel was tied good I would take it right back to the station the way it was, backwards.

So I got back in and turned on my red flashers and drove away. I heard Jim Boynton yell out, So long, Hanger.

But I didn't pay no attention to him. I just kept my eye on the road and kept glancing through both my rear-vision mirrors to see how the Plymouth was riding. It was riding good.

The mirror on my Chevy was almost as big as the wrecker mirrors. I began to wonder if it was too big. Then I thought of Penny for a while, and before I knew it, I was back at the station.

Pete was on the phone, probably talking to his wife, when I dropped the Plymouth in the gravel. There wasn't no one waiting for gas, and Bo was only half busy, smoking a cigarette and keeping his eyes almost shut while he was fixing an inner tube. He didn't even notice me come in.

So I went across the street to the Dairy Freeze.

When Phyllis saw me, she said, Clyde Stout, where on earth you been? Your mother has been phoning you.

Phoning me here? I said.

Yes, when she couldn't get you over to the station, she thought you might be over here drinking a milk shake.

Didn't they tell her I was picking up a wreck?

I don't know, Phyllis said. All I know is she called over here.

Thanks, I said. I turned around and started back to the station.

Let me know if I can help with anything, Phyllis yelled out. But I didn't turn around. I pretended I didn't hear what she said.

Where you been, Hanger? Pete said when I came up.

You know where I been. I been picking up a wreck.

Pete's face got long, and he said, I forgot all about that.

You know, if I had only thought . . . hell, I should have noticed the wrecker wasn't there. And I even took the call for that damned wreck.

He shook his head and looked sad. Things must have been rough at home for Pete to do a dumb thing like that.

Phyllis said I had a call from Mom, I said.

Pete closed his eyes and nodded. That's right, he said. You better call her. I told her I didn't know where you were. I sure am getting forgetful lately.

I phoned home, and Mother said, Clyde? Is that you? She acted like I was calling from the other side of the world and she could hardly remember me.

Yes, it is me, I said.

Clyde, you have another letter. Let's see. It's from Camp Wildwood again. And it says P. Barker, just like the other letter. It's from Penny. Do you want me to open it?

No, I'll read it when I come home, I said. For some reason, my mouth was dry. Even though I had just finished a milk shake.

Do you suppose it's urgent? Mother said.

I don't know, I said.

For a minute we just stood there on either end of the line and I could hear Mother breathing. Then the tire bell rang, and I said I better hang up because a '66 Buick has just drove in.

All right, Clyde, she said.

Then we said good-by, and when I laid the phone back in the receiver, Bo Thompson stepped past and said, Never mind, Hanger, I got it.

8

WHEN WE close up I drove home and got the letter. Mother ask me if it is anything urgent before I even got out of the house with it, but of course I don't know whether it is or not because I haven't opened it, and I told her so.

I went to Chet's place, which is a little hole in the wall lunchroom. There are a few booths in the place and not one of them is comfortable. They all act like they are about to spring up and dump you on the floor or else break down. But Chet is a nice guy and always full of news. And he keeps his soft drinks colder than any place in town, except Dad. Chet wears a sailor hat in the restaurant all the time. He is bald underneath. He is about sixty years old and has a mustache.

I went into Chet's place and there was only Bill Fickle, who owns the Texaco station uptown, there. He was drinking a cup of coffee and eating a piece of Chet's homemade peach pie which is very good.

Root beer? Chet asks when I come in, and I say yes. I take it from his hand and go back to the corner booth. Then I lay down the bottle on the table and slide in the booth. This is the most comfortable booth in Chet's place, only it is cold in the winter with a draft that hits you along the ankles. In the summer, like now, it is just fine.

I take a long drink of root beer and then open Penny's letter. I make a mess out of the envelope because I never know how to open one without tearing it all apart. I am glad I am not a stamp collector. Her letter said,

Dear Clyde,

It is always a pleasure hearing from you and getting news from home. Life is indeed pleasant here at camp and the days pass swiftly by. I have been doing a lot of swimming and playing tennis. Also, I have been, in my spare time, reading *Wuthering Heights* again (for about the fiftieth time!). I simply love that book and as long as I live I will never, never tire of reading it.

I thought your story about Mr. Comisky was interesting. What a strange person he must be! And of course it is so nice that you could earn five dollars so easily.

I am pleased that you have finally gotten a rear vision mirror for your car. I know how much that means to you.

Well, do keep in touch, Clyde. And next time, please try to remember your high school English. Honestly, you write as if you don't know what a past participle *is!*

(I wish letters could show facial expression, and things like that, because I am saying this somewhat in a joking manner, but of course such things can't be conveyed *via* the written word, can they?)

Who in the world is this poet, Farad Karaji, you

mentioned? I have never heard of him, and neither has Beth Holsinger, another counselor here, who is a senior in college and an English major.

Have a Nice Summer,
Penny

Well, Chet said, coming up to my booth and sitting down without asking or anything. Is it good news?

Not so's you would notice, I said.

That's too bad, Chet said. Too bad.

He drummed his fingers on the table between us and looked all around, while I poured some more root beer down my throat.

From one of your friends here in town? Chet finally asked.

It's from Penny Barker, I said.

Say, are you still going with Penny?

I'm not sure, I said.

Chet got up and laughed and slapped me on the shoulder. You know, Hanger, he said, you're quiet, but underneath all that quietness, you have a sharp wit. A sharp wit.

He shook his head back and forth and went over to the cooler to take out a Coke for Jimmy Laird, who had just walked in and who delivers newspapers in this part of town. Jimmy is a very good softball pitcher, even though he is only twelve or thirteen.

He came up to the booth across from mine and sat down, banging the bottle so hard against the table I thought it might break. He look across from where he was sitting and said, Hi, Hanger.

I just look at him a minute, and then I say, Hi.

Chet, I say in a loud voice, has Pete been in here lately?

Not today, I don't think. Why?

Nothing, I said. But I was thinking he must have been here, because Chet had called me Hanger. And so had Jimmy Laird. But there wasn't no use of making a big deal out of it. I once knew a boy who everybody called Low Pants, although I never found out why.

I finished my root beer and left Chet's place. Outside, it was hot again, and I could see the bugs flying under the lights outside the fire station about a hundred yards away. Bruce Flickinger was outside hosing down the cement ramp in front. Last year I fixed the water pump on his '63 Impala. It's got a nice pale green color and dark green upholstery.

I figured Phyllis was off duty out at the Dairy Freeze, so I went on out there to have a milk shake before I went to bed. When I got there and parked my car, I saw Charlotte Barker standing in front of me with two other girls which I didn't know, except one was named Nancy and she had red hair and real long shorts on that fit snug around her knees. Because her legs looked fat, I think.

For a second I was afraid Charlotte was going to say Hello, Hanger, but she just said, Hello, Clyde, have you heard from Penny?

I told her I had just received a letter from her and she was all right.

We stood there and waited for a little bit. It was awful crowded this evening, and the girl named Nancy said so.

By the way, I said to Charlotte. What year MG is that your boy friend has?

I think it's a '63, she said.

I nodded. I thought it was a '63. Only I wasn't sure. I figured it could have been a '64.

Why did you ask? she says.

I didn't know what to answer, so I just said I only wanted to know. Then I remembered her boy friend was from Millford, which is even smaller than our town.

Your boy friend is from Millford, isn't he? I ask her.

That's right, Charlotte said. His father is in business there.

Does he know Mr. Comisky who lives there? I asked.

Charlotte looked thoughtful for a minute. Well, she said, I don't know who he knows, he knows so many people.

This man is a gambler, I told her.

Then her face lit up like somebody pulled a switch and for a second she acted like she was going to grab my arms or something.

Oh, HIM! she said. Oh, I've heard about HIM. Why he's FANTASTIC. He's in and out of mental institutions all the time, and he makes these simply FANTASTIC bets and does all sorts of crazy things. One night he drove his car into the football stadium—nobody knows how he managed to get the car in, unless he bribed somebody—and parked it on the field so the Millford team wouldn't get BEATEN.

Who was that team that was beating Millford? she asked the other girl, not the redhead one.

I don't know, she said.

Well, they couldn't keep that out of the papers, although he's so rich and he's from this old family in Millford, so he can do almost anything and it doesn't get in the papers. But this did. You read about it, didn't you, Nancy?

The redhead girl said yes, she thought she did.

Was that a Caddy he drove out on the football field? I ask her.

A what? Charlotte said.

A Cadillac, Nancy said.

Well, I don't know. I was there with Roger that night and I saw it all. It was FANTASTIC. I mean, it REALLY WAS.

I stared at her, and she said, I don't know whether it was a Cadillac or not, Clyde. Honest, I don't remember. Not only that, I don't think I would know what a Cadillac looks like. Only it's an awful big car. Isn't that right?

I told her it was.

9

WELL, I wasn't too surprise. I drove away from the Dairy Freeze with my milk shake. I didn't know where I was going. I was just driving because I didn't feel like going to bed yet. The night air felt good blowing through my hair and tickling the hairs on my arms. My legs were sweating where they were pressed against the seat, even though I was cool everywhere else.

I wondered if it was worth that five dollars, being called Hanger for the rest of my life. And getting the money from a crazy man. After all, five dollars is not very much when you come right down to it.

A few minutes later and I found myself out at Rigolo's. I pulled the car up into his drive and seen there was nobody about. Rigolo must have taken his wife to the drive-in movies down the road, I thought.

I turned off my engine, noticing it don't idle too bad, considering the trouble I been afraid of, and all of a sudden it is real quiet and cool there in the dark driveway. Rigolo's house is all dark too, only the windows look cool and half lit up because of the moon which is above the hills.

The junk yard seems kind of soft now with nobody

around. And I realize I have never been in a junk yard at night. I am thinking about putting chrome strips down the front of my Chevy. As a matter of fact, I got the idea from that Pontiac where I got the side mirror from. It had chrome strips down the hood, the way those '53 models did, and they looked good. I mean, they didn't have no bubbles in the chrome so far as I could see.

So I climbed Rigolo's gate and walked back into the lot with all them cars. The ones that had glass in the windows just sort of glowed, like they was ice, or something like that. And the cool night air felt good against my arms.

After awhile, I started thinking about Penny. I went several cars beyond the Pontiac, to an old Packard—about 1938 or 1939, I figured—that was setting up on top of a little knoll. I could see all around from that Packard. Probably three or four hundred cars. All different, all old or wrecked, all with different stories behind them. Kind of like people in some ways, I was thinking.

I suppose I was standing up by that Packard for ten minutes, thinking about the cars and Penny, and then I decided to walk on. Things look different at night. I knew most of these cars like the back of my hand, I had come to Rigolo's so many times. But I never seen them at night.

Finally I come to another little knoll where you couldn't even see Rigolo's shed or house. There was an old Buick station wagon there that looked like it was big enough to haul pianos. Its rims were sunk in the ground, clear up to the hubs, it had been there so long.

I climbed up on top and sat there, looking over all the cars around me. Then I thought of that poem by Farad Karaji.

They told me I was alone,
Alone in a whirling world,
Of chance,
Of mystery,
Of servitude and death,
But that was ere
I saw Thee.

After awhile I felt good from everything being so quiet and I walked back down to my car. I noticed that Rigolo and his wife had returned. His Dodge was up by the house and they was a light on in one of the upstairs windows.

When I saw him a few days later and told him about going out into his junk yard at night, he said, Sure. I recognized your car. I figured you were out there looking for something. I knew you'd pay me for anything you got.

10

WHEN I woke up the next morning and went downstairs to breakfast, Mother said, Clyde, do you know we haven't seen Momma for months?

This is what she calls her mother, who lives about twenty-six miles out in the country. I call her that too.

My sister Carol and my little brother Tom were already dressed and out of the house. They eat breakfast before I do, because I work late at night and Mother lets me sleep. When Mother poured the milk over my cereal, she told me that Carol was going to eat lunch at Susie Stalder's house, and she would be gone all day, and Tom was spending the whole day at Gary Peters' house.

Then when I was eating the cereal, Mother said, Do you go in to work at two today, or does Pete want you to come in earlier?

Two, I said.

Then let's you and me go out and see Momma, Mother said.

I didn't say anything, because I didn't want to go, but I couldn't think of any excuse, either. So I just kept quiet and munched on the cereal, which made a lot of noise when I chewed. I don't know what kind it was, because I don't like cereal anyway, but then you have to feed the horse to make him work, as Mother is always saying, and she is right.

How about it? Mother said.

Maybe she won't be home.

Why, Momma never goes ANYWHERE, Mother told me.

I didn't say anything, and Mother shook my shoulder and said, Come on. It'll do you good to take a nice ride in the country, and we'll be back in time for you to go to work. It's a beautiful day for a ride.

Won't she want to see Tom and Carol? I ask her.

That'll be on the next trip, Mother said. It'll give Momma something to look forward to.

I don't know, I said. How about some other time?

Clyde, Mother said in a low voice, it has been almost six months since I have seen my mother. HALF A YEAR.

I could see she was getting work up, so I told her all right, but only if I could drive my Chevy. As a matter of fact, I needed to listen to the engine again. It sounded kind of funny sometimes, as I have mention before one or two times, but other times it sounded just fine.

Not only that, a car needs to get pushed up to sixty-five or seventy now and then, and have its insides blown out good, as Pete is always saying, only I don't ever drive over sixty-five.

When we drive up to her house, I notice that Momma has two wood antique signs now, instead of just one. It is a big white house, with a porch that goes down one side halfway, and all along the front. There are a lot of thick green vines on the side of the porch, and a big hill in back that is covered with trees. I use to go back there when I was a kid and look for copperheads, only I never found one. Everybody was always telling me to watch out for them.

When I shut off the ignition, everything was quiet except for some chickens clucking and a semi grinding up the highway about half a mile away.

She isn't here, Mother said.

Well, we can get out and look, I told her.

But Mother just sat there, and said, We should have called her on the phone to see if she was here.

Maybe she's in back, I said. Working in her garden.

No, Mother said. We'll get out and look, but I have a feeling she isn't here. I have a feeling we've wasted our time.

We got out and went up to the porch, and Mother yelled out, Yoo hoo, Momma. But nobody answered.

What if somebody stopped for antiques, Mother said.

I don't think very many people stop, I said.

No, but what if they DID?

Well, she just wouldn't be home, I told her.

Then Mother said it certainly was nice and cool on the porch, and she ask me if I didn't think that was a wonderful breeze, and I told her I did.

You know, Clyde, she said, this lawn's in bad shape. It certainly needs mowing.

I look at the grass a minute, and saw that it was pretty long.

Then Mother told me that her momma shouldn't have to mow the lawn herself, because she was getting old, and I stood there and look at the grass for a while and listen to the chickens clucking in back.

Then I was surprised all of a sudden to see Momma standing right there by the vines, staring at us. She was wearing a red bandana handkerchief around her hair and a man's shirt rolled up around her elbows and some corduroy pants that belonged to Grampa when he was alive. Her face is real wide and wrinkled, and she use to be fatter than she is now, but she is still fat and sassy, as Mother always says.

When Mother saw her, she said, MOMMA, and her momma said, Well, it looks to me like I got visitors. Who is that big boy, now? Is that you, Clyde?

I said yes, and she walked around to the steps and she and Mother hugged each other, and then Momma grabbed my arm and said, Let's feel your muscle, Clyde, but I didn't want to show her my muscle, so I took my arm away and didn't say anything, and Mother said, He's bashful, Momma, and Momma just kind of looked at me.

Well, what's new back home? she ask Mother, and Mother started right in talking about Mrs. Stevenson next door.

Let's just sit down here on the glider and talk where it's cool, Momma said, and Mother didn't answer, but kept on talking about Mrs. Stevenson right while she was sitting down on the glider and her momma was fussing with some cushions. She didn't miss a word. Neither one of them did.

I was kind of bored, and after awhile, Momma said, Do you want some ice tea, Clyde?

I didn't answer right away, trying to figure out if I did or not, so she turned to Mother and said, Does he want some ice tea?

Mother said, I don't know. Clyde, do you want Momma to make you some ice tea?

I didn't say anything because I hadn't made up my mind yet, and Mother said, Maybe after while, Momma. We just had breakfast an hour ago.

When Mother got through talking about Mrs. Stevenson, Momma said, If I had known you was coming, I would certainly have dressed up a little bit. This is awful, the way I look.

Mother told her she looked just fine, but Momma said, No, I just put on these awful things when I work in the garden. I should dress up now and then, because sometimes an antique customer drops in.

No, you should relax, Mother said. Then she ask Momma if she would like me to mow the lawn for her, and Momma said, Heavens no, let the poor boy relax.

Why, he wouldn't mind, would you, Clyde? Mother ask me, and I told her I wouldn't. As a matter of fact, I would have like it better than just sitting there listening to them talk, but I didn't tell them that.

He certainly is an awful good boy, Momma said.

Where's the lawn mower? Mother ask her, and Momma got up out of the chair and said, I think it's back in the garage. I still have the old hand mower, you know.

It's just a little bitty lawn, Mother said. Clyde can mow it in a jiffy, can't you, Clyde?

When Momma got the lawn mower out, I shoved it through the long grass next to the garden, where there is a line of stones that Grampa painted white years ago, only now they are kind of gray.

Isn't he a strong boy? Momma said, and Mother told her I was.

They stood there and talk and watch me for a few minutes, and then they went inside. After awhile, Momma brought out a pitcher of ice tea, which she knows I like, and we all sat there on the porch and Mother talk about the new tax increase in town, and then about how tough it is on her because Dad is gone so much, driving his truck all over the country, and then she said she hadn't been feeling so good lately and had been in a bad mood a lot of the time. Momma was wearing a dress now, which I had heard Mother say she liked when I come up on the porch.

You've got to expect that, at your time of life, Momma said, and Mother and her just kind of look at each other for a minute and don't say anything.

Then Mother said, I suppose so, but some women have it harder than others, Momma.

That's what they all say, Momma said.

Then Mother talk some more about a lot of other things, and when I got up and started to go back to mowing the lawn, Momma said, Clyde, your mother is sure a talker, isn't she?

I said yes, and she and Mother kind of laugh, only Momma laugh harder. She has a real hearty laugh for an old lady.

She always WAS the talker of the family, Momma said, and Mother said, Now don't tell him that, he might believe you.

Well, it was true, Momma said. Always was, and so far as I can see, still is.

I just have a lot to talk about, Mother said.

I'll say you do.

If you ask me, that's the pot calling the kettle black if I ever heard it, Mother said.

But Momma didn't pay any attention, and then she told

me that Mother could talk a dog off a meat wagon on a hot day, and we all laugh.

Then I went out to the lawn mower again, and when I got to the front, I mowed all around Momma's new antique sign, which she had printed herself, and I remember how she and Mother always joke about her antiques, because she doesn't have hardly any. She has a few bean pots and some old plates and a coffee grinder and a couple old rockers and a table and some candlesticks and things like that. They are all in the shed, piled together, and if anybody stops to buy antiques, it takes them about a half-hour to even get to look inside the shed, and by that time, Momma knows everything about them. Momma admitted to Mother one time that the only reason she has the antique sign up is to get to meet new people. She says antique collectors are very odd people, a lot of them.

When I got through with the lawn, Mother said, Well, Clyde has to go to work after lunch, so I suppose we should be leaving.

Why don't you let me get your lunch, Momma said, but Mother told her we couldn't stay, and then they argued for a while, but finally Mother won, and Momma said, Well, I didn't have nothing very good for you, anyway.

Momma grabbed my hand and put a dollar in it, real quick before I knew what she was doing. I didn't want to take it, but Momma argued a lot, and finally Mother said, Go ahead and take it, Clyde. It'll make her feel better, and Momma said that was true, so I did.

And then we said good-by and drove back to town, and when we got there, Mother made me take another dollar for gas.

11

WHAT I decided on was racing stripes. Three of them, white against the black paint on my car. A lot of them have only two. I could see how neat it would be looking right down along them three stripes when I was behind the wheel. Not that I ever drive fast, because I don't. Bo brags about how fast he drives, and I always say, I never had that Chevy of mine over sixty-five.

It won't go no faster, that's why, Bo says. And then he laughs.

But I tell him it would if I wanted it to, but he only laughs louder, and sometimes Pete joins in, depending on how his wife has been treating him.

For one thing, I wanted the racing stripes on the Chevy by the time Penny got back from camp, and that was only about two weeks away. If they didn't look right, I could paint the car again. I wanted to be sure about something like that.

Of course, I knew they would be all right. So I got some more discount paint and parked the car behind the filling station, where Pete said I could paint the stripes on if I wanted to.

It was a couple days after I went to Rigolo's at night, and I was back there laying on the masking tape so I would get it just right. When I was working with the masking tape, Bo leaned out the back door and said, Hanger, one of these days you're just going to love that car of yours to death. A car is like a woman, you shouldn't love them too hard.

I didn't pay Bo any attention. I know the way he talks and I know how to get along with him. We had a college boy working here at the station last summer for a few weeks and Bo drove him away. Pete never did find out, but I saw what was happening. Bo was always digging him just in the right way, when Pete wasn't looking. Bo didn't like him because he was going to college. But of course that didn't bother me none. Bo didn't bother me neither. He's hardly ever bothered me, except maybe calling me Hanger, which as I mentioned I am getting kind of use to.

Anyway, Bo was pretty good this morning. He covered for me pretty well while I got the first stripe on. Then I took over and poured gas for the next half hour while Bo kind of dogged it and read the paper and got a Coke over at the Dairy Freeze, where Phyllis asked him where I was, and Bo said, Having a love affair with a beat-up piece of merchandise.

I heard Bo tell Pete this when he came back, and both of them laughed and Pete said, Hanger, they threw away the mold when they made you.

Bo shook his head and said, They sure did. Then he said, Been out to Rigolo's lately on a shopping spree?

And then they started right in laughing again, but I didn't pay them no mind, and when I got through filling a Volkswagen with about three teaspoonfuls of gas, as Pete is always saying when he puts gas in a VW, I went around in back to see how the racing stripe was drying, which was not too bad. I was thinking the car would look pretty nice when Penny got home, although it wouldn't be no MG. It would still look pretty. Not bad.

While I was working on the second stripe, Pete leans around the back door and says, Hanger, you got a long-distance phone call.

I stopped and wiped my hands on the old grease rag I had soaked in paint thinner, and went around to the front. The Dairy Freeze was crowded with a bunch of little boys from some Cub pack hike. At least some of them had Cub uniforms on.

When I said hello, I could tell by the sound of my own voice that it was long distance. But then I heard Mr. Comisky's voice say, Is that you, Clyde? So I knew that even though it was supposed to be long distance, it was really only Millford, about twenty-five miles away.

I told Mr. Comisky it was me, and he said he had some plans for me. He asked me if I wanted to make some money, and I told him yes, I did.

I don't mean five dollars, Clyde, he said.

All right, I said. I hoped he meant more than five.

I mean big money, Clyde. But first, you got to promise me something.

What?

You got to promise me you will practice.

Well, I guess so. Practice what?

Practice hanging, Mr. Comisky said.

You mean, that's the way I am going to be making money? I said. I didn't want to say the word hanging.

That's the way, Mr. Comisky told me.

Pete was over at the desk, working on some accounts, but when I looked up at him he was staring at me and I figured he was trying to figure out what I was doing getting a long-distance call.

This is something you can't bluff, Mr. Comisky said. You are going to have to pace yourself. Maybe you will want to hang four or five times a day. Maybe twenty times. I don't know how you are going to manage it. You'll have to use your own judgment, to a great extent. This isn't a well-established sport like sprinting or baseball, where you know how to train a rookie. With this you are just going to have to figure out your own ways to toughen up. But remember, I have a great deal of faith in you—first of all, in your natural ability at hanging free, second, in your honesty in telling me that you will practice . . . I mean, I know you WILL practice, after you say so, and third, I have confidence in your judgment, Clyde . . . in your judgment on how you can best train yourself.

Yes sir, I said.

Remember, it's strength in the hands. Not just gripping strength alone, but holding strength. And then, it's the ability to endure discomfort. I don't think I have to use the word pain. It's more like discomfort. Ache in the shoulders, and that sort of thing. And the fingers crying out to let go. And then too, you have to be stable psychologically, Clyde. One thing I liked about you from the very start is your obvious psychological stability. I mean, you get some guys up there hanging on the bar and they start having visions and Christ knows what all. I don't want any of that. I don't have any use for people who don't have psychological stability.

I was wondering if me thinking about Penny that day on the grease rack was a vision.

Are you still there, Clyde? he ask me.

Yes sir, I said.

It's because of the arteries in your neck, Mr. Comisky told me. When you raise your arms and keep them raised, especially under the pressure of hanging, it clamps the arteries almost shut, sometimes, so that the blood supply to the brain is cut off. Or at least it's cut down to a trickle, and that can give you hallucinations. But do you know what can prevent it?

I told him I didn't.

Will power, Mr. Comisky said.

He waited for me to say something then, but I didn't know what to say, so I didn't.

Will power, he said again. Good old-fashioned intestinal fortitude, or guts. Like in all sports. Right?

I agreed with him.

It separates the men from the boys, Mr. Comisky said. And I define it as psychological stability.

One of the things about talking to Mr. Comisky over the phone was that you could hear him breathing fast and all the time. He must have held the phone awful close to his nose.

Then he started talking about how people laughed at him for trying to start the new sport of free hanging.

You know what they say? he ask me, and I said I didn't.

They say it's goofy. That's what. They don't understand why anybody would want to stand around and watch athletes hang from a bar. And do you know what I tell them?

No, I said.

I tell them, SURE, it's goofy. SURE, it's wacky. But why not have some fun, right?

Just then I hear the tire bell ring, and there is a '66 Buick coming up to the far pump.

Right? Mr. Comisky ask me, and I told him it was.

People don't have vision, he said. They can't see beyond their own noses, and I told him that was true.

Okay, he said. I guess that's about all. Got it straight?

I told him I did.

Think you can remember everything I have said? he ask.

I told him yes sir one more time.

And you believe you can deliver for me?

I guess I can try.

Well, let me put it this way. There's a fellow from Detroit who can hang free for four minutes. Think you can beat that after you do some training?

Pete had laid down his pencil and was staring at me like by now he knew there was something up.

Can you? Mr. Comisky said.

I suppose so, I said.

Just great, Clyde. Just great. And when I say there is money in it, I mean with the kind of bet I am willing to put on you it'll mean two hundred bucks if you can outhang this Detroit flash.

When he said this, Mr. Comisky laugh so loud I had to take the receiver away from my ear.

And after we said good-by, I wandered back to my car thinking all kinds of things. Like, what Charlotte said about him driving his Caddy out on the football field in the middle of a game. I had read about that in the newspaper, but I didn't know Mr. Comisky then.

I kept thinking that that five dollar bill he had give me

was real. Not even Pete could criticize that five dollar bill.

Later on that afternoon, before the big rush around dinnertime, and after I had painted the third stripe on my Chevy, I saw Bo go over to the Dairy Freeze and Pete sit down at his desk again to go over the accounts.

So I grabbed on to the top of the door to the Men's Room and lifted my legs up so they wouldn't be touching the floor. Then I counted one thousand one, one thousand two, one thousand three, until the tire bell rang and I saw a blue '66 Chevy drive up to the far pump, and I went out.

I had only got to one thousand a hundred and eleven, but I could of hung longer. Even though my hands were so numb I almost dropped the gas hose right after I pulled it out of the pump.

The Chevy took thirteen gallons four, and when I filled out the credit card, my fingers were still numb and I could hardly move the pencil right.

Bo come back, and I must of looked at him funny, because he said, What's the matter, Hanger.

But I told him it was none of his business. So he shrugged and went into the office where Pete was working. Bo was eating a cone. It looked like strawberry.

That night it rained and thundered and lightning, but I saw the weather coming, and I put the Chevy in the garage first, before Mother come home from a meeting at the church, so she had to leave her car in the drive.

12

THE NEXT DAY when I come over to the Dairy Freeze, Phyllis makes me a coney and a milk shake, like always, but when she hands them through to me, she says, Clyde Stout, I got to talk to you about something.

What, I told her.

Phyllis is kind of big in the bosom and she is always hugging herself, which she does now, leaning over the service window in the Dairy Freeze. There is nobody else around and I can hear the little colored pennants flapping in the breeze. Phyllis' Ford is parked back at the rear of the lot, so they have room for customers.

I am speaking about your mother, Phyllis said.

What about her?

She is in serious trouble. I just talked to her this morning and since you are her oldest son, I think you should help her.

Help her do what?

Not *do* anything.

She isn't sick, is she? I told Phyllis I never knowed my mother to get sick.

No, not exactly, she told me. But she wants to confide in you. I might tell you that your mother is very proud of you the way you pull your own load even though you don't make much money working for Pete.

Just then Bill Grainger come walking up from his place where he sells Farmall tractors. We all say hi, and Bill orders a chocolate milk shake from Phyllis. She is extra friendly to him, probably because she don't like being interrupted in something so important as what she is talking to me about. Bill Grainger weighs almost three hundred pounds and he always wears a baseball cap.

When he gets his milk shake, he goes over to sit on the shady side of the Freeze, and Phyllis lowers her voice until I can't hardly hear what she is saying. Clyde Stout, she says, I want you to talk to your mother. A mother needs a friend.

Bill comes walking back then and starts kidding Phyllis about last year's county fair stickers she still has pasted to the bumper of her Ford. Her Ford is a '60 and she don't drive it hardly at all. Jim Boynton said she only put four thousand on it last year, but I don't know since I didn't ask her.

She also believes in astrology and every day reads about what the stars say.

While Bill Grainger and she was talking, I went on back to the filling station and we were really busy for a couple of hours, that tire bell going like the bell on a drunken cow, as Pete is always saying.

I kept thinking about them stripes on my Chevy. And it was those couple of hours while I was so busy that I decided they didn't look right, and I would have to paint the car again. I kept thinking about metallic green, which I like and is a very popular color with new cars.

Along about seven o'clock the traffic let up a little. There was Pete and Bo and me handling the station, and a kid about sixteen, name Dean Fetz, who is about six feet three inches tall and very skinny. He is still in high school and he plays basketball, but not very good.

Anyway, about seven o'clock Bo was taking care of a Chevy customer (a '64, if I remember right), and Pete was eating an egg salad sandwich and drinking a 7-Up. I didn't know what Dean Fetz was doing, but he was out of sight, so I grabbed on to the edge of the Men's Room door and hung a while. Then I saw Dean standing right behind me, and he said, What are you doing, Hanger?

I told him I was stretching my muscles.

Just then, Bo comes up and says, What was old Hanger doing, Dean?

I told him I was stretching my muscles, I said.

Bo looked at me with a grin and says, That hanging must be habit forming. Then he turned back to Dean and says, Was he hanging, Dean?

That's what I was doing, I said. And the next time you want to know what I am doing, I am the one to ask. Meanwhile, go piss up the grease rack.

As you can tell, I was very angry because I don't talk that way very often, unless I am. I have always tried to never talk dirty the way Bo and Jim Boynton always do, for instance.

Old Bo was laughing all over the place. He even had to lean against the hydraulic jack, which he forgot to put back where it belongs. Then he had to go in to tell Pete and a couple seconds later Pete come around the corner from his office with his cheeks bulged out with egg salad sandwich and almost choking from a laugh he can't get out because his mouth is too full.

Well, they laugh awhile and Dean kind of laughs too, only he is a little bit reserved, like I am usually, and doesn't make too much out of it. After awhile, though, Pete and Bo got him to try his hand at hanging. They told him I done it for two minutes and earned five dollars, maybe he would like to try it. Only they didn't say anything about giving him five dollars.

So they lowered the grease rack for him to grab on to, just like Pete did for me, and Dean hung up there for one minute and fourteen seconds and then he just kind of gasped and let go. It is an awful strain and Mr. Comisky says you got to have a high threshold of pain as well as strong hands. You got to be tough. By which he means you can't be too sensitive, like yelling out when you slice your knuckle to the bone with a tire tool, the way I did that day I first met Mr. Comisky. Only I didn't yell out, because I don't make a big thing out of a little cut.

Later on, Bo said, I wonder if I could hang on to that thing for two minutes. And Pete told him to go ahead, so Bo tried it but let go in less than a minute. That is when you begin to think your arms are going to pull out of their sockets. So I didn't blame him for letting go in less than a minute.

So they all said I was the champion hanger and deserved the title. Which seemed to strike them all the funnier. Especially when I pointed out to them that after all, you can't beat the best. And if you really stop to think about it, baseball or broad jumping is just as silly as hanging. Like Mr. Comisky told me one time on the telephone.

Bo said the only broad jumping he liked to do was in bed and Pete laugh like he was going to lose his egg salad.

Later on when I thought of that conversation, I was

kind of sorry I had brag like that. I kept hearing myself say, You can't beat the best, and I felt like a fool. Because anybody can see it is a crazy thing, hanging. And I could understand that it would take a crazy man to invent it as an athletic event.

13

I WAS sweeping up the garage with the long push broom when I see a clean '63 Corvette come in. We had just cut the lights and Pete was closing up the cash register. The lights flashed through the windows of the garage doors and then the Corvette stopped right in front.

I was surprise to see Jim Boynton walk out of the car. I laid down the push broom and lifted the door. I hadn't seen Jim for about a week.

Is that yours? I ask.

And he says, What do you think of it?

Pretty nice, I said. I tried to sound kind of bored, but it was an awful nice car. It looked like it had all the extras. And it had been babied, you could tell.

Only eighteen thousand miles, Jim said.

Pretty nice, I said. When did you get it?

Last week. Right after I saw you drag that '64 Plymouth out of the ditch. Up on 123. Remember?

Sure, I told him.

Come on and take a ride with me, he said. I want to talk to you anyway.

Wait a couple minutes, I said. We are just closing up.

So Jim got back in the Corvette and raced the engine a couple of times so I could hear it. And it sounded pretty good, I will have to admit.

When I finished, I went out and got in the car and Jim took off past the drive-in movie, on the road to Rigolo's. He pushed it up to seventy-five by the city limits, figuring the traffic was light.

I don't never drive fast like that, and Jim knows it. But I don't say nothing when other people do. I figure that is their business, like driving with good sense is mine.

Bo drives the fastest I ever seen. He has got two speed tickets in the past three years and the next time he will have his license suspended.

As Jim was driving along, we comment on the Corvette, which is a nice buy, I told him. It hangs the curves real good and has good response, I tell him.

But then Jim starts talking about something else. He says, Hanger, I don't know of anybody who doesn't like you.

I figured that was a funny thing to say, and I didn't know what to say back to him, so I just kept quiet.

But I guess he didn't expect me to give him an answer.

And that is why I want to set you straight on something, he said. Because I don't want to see a nice guy like you get hurt. You know what I mean?

I told him I did. But really I didn't, because I didn't have any idea what he was talking about.

Last weekend, he said, I went up to Camp Wildwood to see Judy. That was Judy Wechsler, and now I began to see what he was leading up to.

And Judy told me a few things about Penny, Jim said.

Things were quiet a couple seconds while Jim passed a Rambler station wagon, '61 or '62, I'm not sure which, because I was worried about what Jim was going to tell me.

Go on, I said to him.

Well, I guess Penny has been talking a lot about you to the girls up there. And . . . goddammit, Hanger, let me just tell you to forget about her. Okay? I won't give you all the details, but believe me, Penny is not on your side. She doesn't like you for a boy friend, if you know what I mean.

Yes, I said. She told me that in a letter.

Well, why don't you just quit writing to her. You know, Judy thinks you are a nice person, and so do some of the other girls up there, and they are getting pretty goddam tired of hearing Penny laugh about the English you use and things like that.

I didn't say anything, and we drove on for a few minutes and then passed a '59 Ford that had a busted muffler.

Okay? Jim said, when the car had straightened out. He was doing about eighty now. But the road was pretty good.

Okay, I told him.

Then we drove along kind of quiet for a while, with just the headlights of cars coming the other way flashing in our eyes now and then. Jim slowed down to seventy, which is still fast for night, but he is a good driver and I relax quite a bit and thought about Penny.

I have notice that one of the best times to talk to somebody is when you are driving in a car, because then you don't have to look at them, but just at things up ahead, like the trees and fence posts going past. And cars coming the other way.

And after awhile Jim Boynton says to me, Clyde, you are a funny guy. I was thinking about you the other day.

What were you thinking? I ask him.

Oh, about the kind of guy you are. You know something?

What?

You are too nice a guy to let people walk over you the way they do.

I don't let them walk over me, I told him.

Yes you do, Jim said. Like that squirrelly old broad at the Dairy Freeze.

I knew he was talking about Phyllis, but I didn't say her name. I just said, She's not so bad.

I was in the station the other day, having Pete size up a Riviera I was thinking of buying.

Pete said you were thinking about a Riviera. It was a nice car, he told me.

Yes, but this Corvette doesn't have the miles on it. Anyway, Pete was saying she is always getting you over there to the Dairy Freeze to give you advice and bawl you out.

Yes, but she has a good heart, I said.

Then Jim said a word which I won't write down, and he called her a squirrelly old broad again, and went on to tell me that people were always shoving me around, and I was too nice a guy to let them do it.

He talked on for a pretty long time and told me it was about time for me to wake up and realize how everybody was treating me. He said you got to stand up for yourself in this world, and he would never let a goofy old broad like Phyllis shove him around, if it was the last thing he ever did.

After he had talk a while, we came into Purserville, where there was a Dairy Queen, not a Dairy Freeze, and had milk shakes, which Jim insisted on paying for, and I let him.

When we finished our milk shakes, we drove back and didn't talk much. Jim was driving slower now, and we talked about other things. I told him I had made up my mind to paint my Chevy again, and get rid of the racing stripes. He said that was a good idea. He didn't think they looked right either.

14

MOTHER WAS waiting up when I pulled the Chevy in the drive. She was sitting out on the patio in back, right in the dark, smoking a cigarette. I helped Dad make that patio three years before, when I was just about to turn sixteen. I remember because I was working on my sixteenth birthday and Dad said I didn't have to, but I went ahead anyway because I always did like to work. Better than anything else. Especially doing things with my hands. I rebuilt a Chevy engine when I was seventeen, just a little over a year ago. All by myself, only Pete gave me a few hints. That was a '50 Chevy I had, before I got my '56.

Mother was sitting there smoking a cigarette and I could tell she was waiting for me. When I came up, she ask me where I been, and I told her up to Purserville with Jim Boynton, and she said, Did he drive fast? And I said, About usual.

Clyde, she said, sit down for a minute, will you?

I did. I sat down on the brick wall we made around the patio. It is about two feet high, six bricks high, anyway, whatever that is.

Clyde, she says, did Phyllis talk to you today?

Yes.

About me?

I told her she did.

I didn't want her to tell you, Clyde. But I had to tell somebody, and Phyllis is an awful good friend. She has her ways, and she does talk a lot, but Clyde, she has a wonderful heart. A wonderful heart.

An airplane flew over then, very high. It seemed funny to see it flying over so late at night. Its red and green lights blinked on and off and in a minute it was gone. I don't know whether Mother was watching it or not.

Clyde, she said, we have had our troubles. Our family has. You know, with Judith and all.

Yes, I told her. And then I ask her if she is sick or something, and she started to cry. I didn't know what to do. I hadn't seen her cry for a long time.

No, she said after awhile, I am not sick. But I am lonely and afraid and I don't know what all is wrong. I keep thinking about your father.

What about him? I said.

Why, he is away all the time. Don't you know how hard it is on a woman when her husband is away all the time?

Yes, I said, but I suppose it is hard on him too.

That's one thing that worries me, Mother said. And her voice got different when she said this.

I didn't say anything, and then she took a deep breath and said, It isn't always hard on a man. Do you know what I mean?

I told her I did, and I did.

The other day, my mother said, her voice sounding kind of low like she was afraid the bushes would hear, I read this article about a man who was a traveling salesman and had two wives.

I didn't know what to say to that, and all of a sudden

Mother starts crying again, so loud she wouldn't have heard me even if I had tried to say something.

When she quieted down a little, I said, Mother, don't take it so hard because I am sure Dad is faithful.

Do you really think so, Clyde? she ask me, and I told her I did. She ask me the same question about four times, until I was so sleepy I could hardly keep my head up. But I kept answering her that I did really think he was faithful and that he did not have another family someplace.

For all we know, he does, Mother kept saying.

But I told her that was very rare and that is why the newspapers printed it when it happened.

Mother seemed to feel better. Once or twice, she said, Yes, but he is away so much of the time. A married man shouldn't spend so much time away.

That is his job, I told her.

Yes, but it didn't use to be this way, she said. When he was working for Consolidated.

Yes, but he didn't make the money he is making now, I told her.

That's right, Mother said. And Judith costs us a lot of money, because your father is proud and wants to pay everything he can to keep her doctored and taken care of.

Mother blew her nose once or twice and then she told me that she felt a lot better because she knew how close Dad and I always was and she figured I would know if he had another family someplace or a mistress.

I am awfully glad Phyllis told you, Mother said, squeezing my arm. You know, she certainly has a wonderful heart. And she has *her* troubles too, with that crazy husband of hers, who won't do a thing.

I told her she certainly did, and that I was sure everything was all right. Then I went to bed. Only before I went to sleep, I thought of certain things Dad had said here and there, and I wasn't as sure as I pretended to Mother. I mean, I didn't think he had another family or anything like that, but I wasn't so sure he didn't maybe cheat on Mother now and then. I am not saying he did, but I overheard him and Rex Porter, who is also a cross-country driver, only not for J. T. Oakes, talking one time, and . . . well, there is no point in going over that. He is a pretty good father when all is said and done. He works hard, and I really don't think he drinks. Even when he is away from home. At least not very much, if he does.

15

THE NEXT WEEK I got two letters and painted the racing stripes out so you could hardly notice it. I had enough black lacquer left from painting the car before. It looked a lot better with the racing stripes off, and I was glad because after thinking about it, Penny would of hated them.

The first letter I got was on the day after my nineteenth birthday and it was from Dad. There was also a ten dollar check which just about knocked me off my chair.

Here was his letter.

Old Partner,

It seems to me I forgot your birthday the last two or three years and your mother put a bug in my ear last time I was home, so I am sending you ten dollars TO SPEND ON YOURSELF. Notice those big letters, big boy. Your dad really means it.

I am proud that you are pulling your own weight and wish you a happy birthday.

See you next month.

Dad

Mother gave me five dollars, for gas, she said, or anything else I wanted to do with it. She also gave me one of them little hula dolls that shake their hips when your car swerves or hits a little bump. That kind of surprise me, especially after our talk the other night. But Mother laughed when she gave it to me and said it would really liven up the car. Which it does. I am only glad Bo doesn't have it in his car, or he would get in a wreck all the time, from watching the hula doll instead of the road.

The next time I saw Phyllis, she was making up a big order of barbecue sandwiches and orange drinks for a stranger who I never saw before. He had his family in a pale green '67 Buick.

When she had taken care of him, Phyllis come up to the window and she said, Clyde Stout, I am proud of you for talking to your mother and calming her down. You have made her feel a lot better.

All the time she was getting my milk shake and coney island, she kept talking about that, and what a trial it is for a woman to go through the change of life, which to tell you the truth is something I never thought of.

When I finished lunch, I went back to the station and did some hanging. Pete and Bo didn't say too much about my hanging now, so I did it out in the open. Right from the grease rack, because the Men's Room door didn't work too good. Of course I didn't do it if there was work to do or there was customers around. The minute that tire bell would ring, I would drop to the floor and be ready to go out and pump gas.

Bo would sometimes poke me in the ribs to make me drop, but I am not ticklish, or sensitive in other ways, so it never bothered me, and pretty soon Bo stopped poking me because it wasn't doing no good anyway.

I was planning to spend the ten dollars Dad sent me

out at Rigolo's and use the five mother give me for gas. Or maybe I should save it until I had enough for a metallic green paint job. I only wish that Rigolo had a good grill for a '56 Chevy, because that was the worst part of my car. Maybe I would write a letter to several junk yards in the state and ask if they have one.

Jim Boynton come in the station and filled up with gas, and him and Bo and me had some soft drinks and talked awhile. Things were slow right then, and Pete was in the office looking at some ads for a new motor oil they are making. The phone rang and then Pete came to the door and said, Hanger, it is for you. Your mother, I think.

So I went in and answered the phone and it was my mother, and she was crying. I was afraid it was something to do with the other night when she had told me how worried she was about Dad.

But it wasn't. It was only a notice from my draft board, telling me that I was to report for induction into the army. They gave me a couple weeks to settle my affairs, the letter said. When I hung up and told the fellows, they all said, Well, I'll be goddam.

That was the second letter I got that week.

They didn't tease me none all the rest of that afternoon. Bo brought me an extra-thick milk shake and a coney back from the Dairy Freeze, along with a message from Phyllis to keep my chin up. I figured she had found out about it right after I did, because either Mother called her or Bo told her. Maybe both.

Pete was really sad because I was going into the army. After I finished my milk shake and coney island, he said, Hanger, why don't you haulass out of here and go out to Rigolo's and spend that ten dollars your daddy give you.

I didn't answer him right away and he act like he was almost mad at me. Go on, he said, before it gets dark and you can't see what kind of junk you are getting.

I turned to Bo and Dean Fetz, who had just come in to work, and they was just standing there staring at me.

Get your ass out of here, Pete said, and buy yourself something you really like for that goddam wreck of yours.

So I went. I never seen Pete so worked up. You would have thought it was him going into the army. I suppose he was on edge too, because of his wife. Sometimes he calls her a fourteen carat bitch, but he never says anything about leaving her.

I got in my Chevy and drove kind of slow out past the drive-in and around the curve to Rigolo's. Only I didn't feel excited like I usually do. For one thing, I didn't like the way Pete was acting. He didn't have to say that I was going to buy junk, and he didn't have to call my Chevy a wreck, because it is not.

Rigolo was down on his hands and knees filing the edge of a fender he had taken off a Chrysler.

When I come up, he grunts and sits back on the ground, and says, Hi there, Hanger. I didn't see you come up.

Now that Rigolo was calling me Hanger, I suppose everybody in town, except maybe Phyllis and Mother, would be calling me that.

I ask Rigolo if he thought maybe I could put a '58 Plymouth grill on my Chevy.

He frowns for a minute and then belches, like he always does, because he has a bad stomach. Then he says, No, Clyde, I don't think it would work. Too much cutting.

I was glad he had called me Clyde.

He saw me looking over in the junk yard, and he knew I wanted to look around, just because I enjoyed it. So he said, Why don't you go take a look anyway. There's a '58 Plymouth with a solid grill in the far corner someplace.

I know, I said. I seen it.

When I went through the gate, Rigolo said, If anybody could make it work though, it would be you, Hanger.

That was a nice thing for Rigolo to say, and I could hardly keep from kind of grinning while I was walking back to take a look here and there. I knew exactly what that Plymouth looked like, so there was no point in going to see it again. It had been sideswiped a couple of years ago, and I could remember every dent in the body. The grill was almost perfect, but I knew I couldn't fit it on my Chevy. I was just asking Rigolo that question to pass the time of day. And I think he knew I knew. Because it was a simple question and kind of foolish.

When I left, Rigolo was still on the ground sanding that Chrysler fender, and I told him I had been drafted. He stood up and shook hands with me and told me good luck.

I drove back to town thinking what a good guy old Rigolo was, and Pete too, in spite of this afternoon. And even Bo, when you come down to it. And I couldn't forget Jim Boynton, or Phyllis, who had a wonderful heart, even though she did talk too much. Maybe not Bo too much though. He wasn't very good natured. Dean Fetz seemed to be a pretty nice guy though.

Of course, I always feel good after a visit to Rigolo's. I like to stand there and look over them wrecked cars and think of how many funny looking cars that really worked you could make out of the parts that were lying there and collecting rust. It was like they was just waiting for somebody to come and put them together in new ways and make them work.

Also I liked to do what Rigolo was doing, I mean filing down through the rust of an old piece of metal, and through the old paint too, until you come to the shiny metal itself, which is just beautiful it is so smooth and bright. And I like to think it has been there all the time underneath the rust and the dull old paint which people are always talking about as being so ugly.

16

ALL THE WAY back from Rigolo's I was thinking of how surprise Pete and Bo and Dean Fetz would be that I hadn't bought nothing. I would just explain to them that I didn't see exactly what I want, and I don't believe in wasting money.

Then for a while I thought of Penny and what Jim Boynton had told me about her. I could see her face when I close my eyes. Just like that day I was hanging from the grease rack, and when Mr. Comisky had said, One minute is over, I had seen Penny's face there before me, because my eyes are closed.

I hadn't had any more visions since then, even though I had hung over three and a half minutes on the rack the day before. Nobody was around to bother me then and I could concentrate. Even though I am not ticklish or sensitive when it comes to Bo jabbing me in the ribs with his finger while I am hanging from the grease rack, I still don't like for him to be around when I am hanging.

It was after dark when I pulled up to the station, and there were three cars at the pumps. Bo and Dean Fetz were pumping for two of them and Pete was inside the garage, lifting the dip stick out of a '64 Olds.

When Pete saw me, he didn't even ask me if I got anything, like I thought he would do. He just said, There was a long-distance phone call for you, Hanger. You're supposed to call back. The number's in there on the pad.

I look on the pad and it said I was supposed to call Operator 2 at Rushville, so I did, and she put me through to a Millford number, and it was Mr. Comisky again.

Clyde, he said, how is the hanging?

Pretty good, I told him.

What is your best? he ask me.

Three and a half minutes, I said.

He was quiet a minute, and then he says, Was that from the grease rack? And I told him it was.

Good, he said. You should be able to beat that on a regular bar. Don't you think? I mean, you can grip a regular bar, but you can't really grip that grease rack. Not like you can a bar.

I told him that was possible, so he said he wanted me to come down to his place in the afternoon on the day of the meet if I could get off.

I went and ask Pete, and he said yes, I could have that afternoon off if I wanted it. He told me that between now and the minute I went into the army, I could call my own shots and have any time off I wanted.

So I told Mr. Comisky and he said that was fine. Then he told me how to get to his place near Millford, and told me not to eat too much, on the day of the match, but have plenty of strength anyway. Also to do all the hanging I could so I would be in tiptop condition. And to be there at about 2:30, sharp, because that was when the four minute man from Detroit was supposed to show up.

I told him I would be there.

That night I went home and Mother was asleep, so I didn't talk to her, but went into my bedroom instead and just happened to look at the book of poetry by Farad Karaji, *Singing on the Wings of Time,* which I hadn't looked at for a long time.

I remember what my English teacher, Miss Temple, had said, that you should make friends with a poem if you kind of like it, even if you do not understand it yet. A poem, she said, is like a person who you maybe do not understand completely at first, but after awhile, you do, learning all the person's ways and ideas.

So I sat on my bed in my undershorts, because it was very hot in my bedroom, and I opened Mr. Karaji's book of poems. I wondered why Penny had never heard of him. Then I read some poems, the first of which went this way,

DESTINY

Never in the smoke of eternity
Relieved of it, will he be
(The perishing Fall
Of winters' snowy echoes),
Each hero, unnaturally tall,
Steps forward like a brave tree,
And into his destiny grows.

Then I read this one,

THAT WHICH TOLLS AT NIGHT

Love.
The word tolls like a bell
In the night of my longing
Penetrating the perfume
Of my dreams,
But only to tell me
I am alone.

And this one which I kept thinking of now and then, partly because the first line made me think of a Santa Claus song I use to hear when I was a kid,

MARTYROS

Far away on the rooftops
Of the world
A single solitary bird,
No heavier than the petal
Of a sleepy flower,
Falls,
And I feel the impact
Of its tiny body
In the tendons of my arm,
The flesh of my shoulders,
And in the tenderest
Loneliness
Of my heart.

I kept forgetting the title of that last poem, which was a word I didn't understand anyway, and I always thought of it as the Far Away on the Rooftops poem. I remembered the rest of it because I read it about six or seven times, like Miss Temple told us to do, and after that I remember all the words. Even though I forgot the title.

I kept thinking of that bird and Mr. Karaji, the poet, who was so sensitive he let it bother him when the bird fell down, even though the bird fell down on the other side of the world.

Mr. Karaji would certainly not make a very good hanger, I thought.

I wrote down a few things in my diary before I went to sleep.

17

THE NEXT MORNING, Mother told me her automatic washer had broke down and she ask me if I would take some things out to the laundromat, which I did. The laundromat is about a quarter-mile beyond the filling station, and you can see the sign from the Dairy Freeze, only you can't see it from the station because of Bill Grainger's Farmall Tractor sign.

I put all the things in one of the washers and sat there for a while reading an old *Sports Afield* magazine, which was kind of dirty and coming apart, and then I got thirsty and wonder if I wanted a root beer from the laundromat or a milk shake from the Dairy Freeze. It seemed kind of early for a milk shake, but I decided to go down and get one anyway, only I was hoping Phyllis wouldn't start talking because she practically never stopped when she got started.

I drove the Chevy down, even though it was only a quarter-mile, like I said, and when I walk up to the window, there was no one there. For a minute I just stood there looking, then Phyllis raised her head up from down below where she had been wiping up the floor. Her face was red because she had been stooping over.

Oh, Clyde, it's you, she said, and I told her it was.

Are you ready? she ask me.

For what? I said.

Now, Clyde, don't start that.

I just stood there and looked at the big strip of paper on the window, listing all the Dairy Freeze flavors. I was sorry I had come, because Phyllis was mad about something again.

Didn't your mother tell you? she ask me.

Tell me what? I said.

About helping my husband with the dining room suit.

No she didn't, I said.

Phyllis sighed and stared at me very hard.

She said you would be glad to help; so I told Phil you would be there.

Be where?

At the auction house. I went to the auction Wednesday, and I bought this huge dining room suit. It's oak and very heavy, so I called your mother last night to see if you could give Phil a hand, and she said she'd tell you and you'd be glad to.

It's the first time I've heard about it.

Well, she should have ask you, Phyllis said, and I told her that was true.

Well, would you? she ask me, and I said I would.

You'd better hurry, then. Phil is probably out there now. He rented a U-Haul trailer.

I left some clothes up in the laundromat, I told her, and Phyllis said she would try to call her husband and tell him to wait for me. Then she said she didn't know why she had bid on the dining room suit, but she had. Her horoscope for that day had said it was a time of opportunity, and she told me all she could think about was that dining room suit.

I told her I would go help her husband as soon as I got the clothes out, and Phyllis said thanks and she didn't know what business she had buying the old junk anyway, since she already had a decent dining room suit. But now that she had bought it, she wasn't going to give up on it.

I told her that's the way things happen sometimes, and she said it was nice of me to help out and she hope she could return the favor some day. And then she reminded me not to forget my mother, which I told her I wouldn't do.

After I took the clothes back home, I went out to the auction house, which is a big gray shingle barn at the edge of town. It belongs to Perry Wilson, who is the brother of Bert, who I got the paint for my Chevy from. Phyllis' husband was sitting there on the end of the U-Haul trailer with his elbows on his knees and chewing gum. His face is real red and square, and he is always in a bad mood.

Well, I see you made it, he told me, and I said I had.

I was just beginning to enjoy the rest, he said.

I didn't say anything, but I thought that was a funny thing for him to say, since he didn't ever work anyway.

After he said this, he just sat there and chewed his gum a while and looked over my head at the sky. I saw Perry Wilson's '47 Ford panel truck, which he says he has put two hundred thousand miles on without changing the oil once. Perry wasn't around anywhere, but there was a collie lying in the shade and panting. I don't know who it belonged to.

My friend, Phyllis' husband told me, our fate awaits.

When I looked at him, he pointed at a table and some chairs sitting outside, up next to the big sliding door of the auction house.

But he didn't move. He just took a deep breath and blew it out slow, like he was tired and trying to blow out a candle. He still hadn't even taken his elbows off his knees, and I was figuring he must be about the laziest person in the world, only Phyllis says he is just sick and has a bad attitude.

Then he ask me why Phyllis had bought a dining room suit, when they already have one, and I told him I didn't know.

It's a waste of money, he said. And a waste of energy.

That's a big table, I told him.

He nodded and said, Big enough for a family of twelve, but old Phyllis wouldn't notice a thing like that. Her horoscope said OPPORTUNITY and old Phyllis starts bidding. You know what she bought one time, just because her horoscope said OPPORTUNITY?

I told him no, and he hit both of his knees with his fists and said, AN ANTIQUE WASHING MACHINE.

I couldn't remember ever seeing one, so I didn't know what it was like, but I didn't say anything, because Phyllis' husband was awful sensitive sometimes and very hard to talk to.

He took another deep breath and stood up then, and we walked over to the dining room suit. I was wondering why he hadn't backed the U-Haul trailer right up next to it, and when he grabbed the first chair and started to carry it back, I ask him about it.

He looked mad at first and just threw the chair down on

the ground. Then he stood there for a minute and finally said, All right, if that's the way you want to do it.

So he got in the car and then started backing the U-Haul trailer all over Perry Wilson's lot. You could tell he had never back a trailer because he was always turning the wheel wrong, making the trailer jackknife.

Finally he got out of the car and let the door swing open.

That's close enough now, he said.

I just stood there and look at the car, because now it was farther away than when he started, but I didn't say anything because I could tell he was mad at something.

He picked up the gate of the trailer, which he had run over twice, and threw it aside.

How about a Pepsi? he said, dusting his hands together, like he had got them dirty, and I told him okay.

He put his hands in his pocket and turn around to the trailer and said, I suppose you can pull it up a little closer than that, if you want to. Go ahead. I'll let you drive it while I'm getting the Pepsis.

Then he went in to the auction barn where they have a big Pepsi cooler, and I went out to his car, which was about fifty yards away, and backed the trailer up next to the dining room suit.

When he came back out, Phyllis' husband was carrying two cold Pepsis, and we stood there in the sun and drank them. He didn't seem to notice that the trailer was in a different place.

So we loaded everything on the trailer, and before he drove away, he said he was disgusted because Phyllis didn't think he had anything better to do than fool around with junk like that.

Then he started talking about what a crooked town this was, and how a man named Ted Walker had gypped him out of several thousand dollars. I had never heard of Ted Walker, but Phyllis' husband said he was rich and was always telling the mayor what to do.

Then Phyllis' husband told me that everybody was crooked and had their price and that it was impossible to keep sane if you had any brains at all.

Then he started talking about the idle rich, and how they didn't deserve to have so much money, and then talked about some man he knew who wasn't married and lived with his mother and was nothing but a drag on society.

What is a bastard like that good for? he ask me, and I didn't answer him, but he kept on asking me until I said I didn't know.

You're damned right you don't know, Phyllis' husband told me. Because he isn't good for anything.

I didn't know it at the time, but he was probably talking about Mr. Comisky.

Then he talk about a lot of other things, but I didn't pay much attention, because I didn't know why he was telling me about them. Also, I didn't know what he was talking about half the time, because he jumped around so much, from one thing to another.

Finally he got finished and drove away, telling me thanks, and I went home too.

When I got home, Mother told me, Did you get in touch with Phyllis' husband? and I told her I had.

I forgot to tell you she called, Mother said. I was so wrapped up in the washer, that I forgot to tell you. But I'm glad you got in touch with her. Was it a nice dining room suit?

It was okay, I said.

Phyllis said it was okay, Mother said, and I told her it was.

Then she said, Fred Polcher told me he would be by this afternoon.

I just look at Mother, and she said, You know, to fix my washer, and I said, Oh, yes.

18

THE NEXT DAY I had a vision.

We had our regular noon hour rush and then the cars stop coming all of a sudden, like somebody pulled the plug, as Pete says. Then Pete says, It's siesta time, like he does sometimes. Pete got out an egg salad sandwich and a 7-Up out of the cooler, and Bo went over to the Dairy Freeze to kid with Phyllis and I took care of a '60 Plymouth that come in. Its tailpipe was all rusty and dragging on the cement. It was a couple farm boys from up near Purserville. I have seen them around here and there.

When I finish with the Plymouth, which only took a dollar's worth of regular, cash, I went back into the garage. It was a very hot day and we sure needed rain. That is what everybody was talking about, how much we needed rain, but what do you expect in August?

There was nothing particular to do except maybe sweep up, but I figured we could do that later, so I pulled the hydraulic lever and raised the grease rack.

Pete must of had his mouth empty of egg salad because he heard the rack go up and he yelled out, Have a nice hang, but I didn't give him an answer because no answer was needed.

I jumped up a little bit and grabbed on and looked at

my wrist watch, which has a second hand on it. It was about ten seconds till. So I just kind of relaxed and hung there a couple minutes, and then my arms begin to get uncomfortable, but I didn't move because that is against the rules. Mr. Comisky said you can't shrug your shoulders or nothing like that because that rests you. Like a trapeze artist, he can hang longer because he is moving his muscles and straining them, which increases the circulation and rests them in a way. It is not like free hanging, which is tougher on you.

I saw the second hand go around three minutes, and then something funny begin to happen, only I didn't let go. It was like the color of the whole garage turn kind of tan. A real pale tan, maybe like a dusty road. Except everything was like that, and I could not make out the rivets on the steel beams overhead, or the hydraulic hoses that are strung along the ceiling of the garage, and the water pipes.

Then it was like the whole garage was the inside of a bubble from bubble gum that somebody is blowing up. It just swelled up, and I thought, This is the way it is, exactly, if I was inside a piece of bubble gum and somebody was blowing it up.

Then it popped, but without making no noise at all, and it was like late at night, and there was a long skinny icicle pointing straight up into the air, like a million miles beyond earth. Very thin and very bright. Only everything else was dark. And it was like I could hear a big wind blowing outside, only I was still in some kind of cave, or maybe it was that big bubble I had thought about before.

I don't know how long I hung there because I lost count. What I do remember is Pete crumpling up the sack his wife packs his egg salad sandwich in. He always makes a lot of noise doing that. One day, Bo just about jumped out of his pants when he was sitting there beside Pete and Pete all of a sudden cracks his paper bag up into a ball and tosses it in the green plastic wastebasket we keep beside the cash register. But then Bo is awful nervous anyway, and jumps at the least thing. I can imagine what would happen if Bo was hanging from the grease rack and I come along and jab him in the ribs. He would go off like a bomb.

Anyway, I let go and hit the cement and found out where I was. The vision had disappeared. I did not say anything to Pete about it.

Right then Bo comes in and says, Hanger, Phyllis was asking about you. She says she wants to talk to you.

When doesn't she want to talk to me? I ask.

Bo and Pete kind of look at me when I say this, because I don't talk like this very much. But I was still feeling kind of funny because of the vision.

She's not a bad old girl, Bo said.

Nobody said she is a bad old girl, I told him.

What's got into you, Hanger? Bo ask.

None of your business.

You don't usually snap a guy's head off, Bo said. He look like his feelings were hurt, but I didn't say anything else. But when I turn away, I saw Pete nudge him with his elbow, and Bo got quiet. Later on that afternoon I heard Pete tell him that I was upset about going into the army. But that wasn't true, I was just still shaky from the vision. But of course I couldn't tell them about the vision, so I just kept still and let them think I was worried about the army.

Actually, I was kind of looking forward to it. I was hoping they would put me in the mechanic's corps where I would work on trucks and jeeps and things like that. I figured after a few years in the army I would be a first-rate mechanic, which Pete sometimes says I am now, but I figure he is only complimenting me to make me feel good.

The only thing I would miss would be Penny.

I wondered what the poet, Mr. Karaji, would do if he had a vision like the one I had that afternoon.

19

I TOLD MYSELF, I am nineteen years old and I am pulling my own load, so there is no reason I should not do what I want to do with my own money. Because nobody else has to know about it.

I took the ten dollars Dad had sent me for my birthday present, and I went up to Hillary's Drug Store. This was when Pete thought I was out to supper because I had told him I was going to supper. The station was pretty busy.

Annabelle was there, waiting on a fat woman who was holding a little hairy dog on a leash. The dog kept winding its leash around the woman and sniffing at a stack of bath salts that were on special, seventy-nine cents. Annabelle was tired of waiting on the woman, it look like, because she is leaning on her elbows on the glass counter. She acted like her legs had give way and all she had to hold herself up with was her elbows. The fat woman was standing there with her legs apart and that little dog straining at the leash which she don't even feel, she is so big and heavy.

When the fat woman was through, Annabelle looked at me and said, Are you here again? and I told her I was and I wanted to buy that $4.95 make-up kit she showed me the other night, about a week ago.

Annabelle remembered, and she sold it to me, and when she was putting it in a sack, who should walk in but Rigolo.

Hello there, Hanger, he says to me, and I said hello.

Buying something for the army? he said.

I told him it was for a friend.

Rigolo kind of laugh and then he goes back to the prescription counter to get some milk of magnesia tablets, which he practically lives on, his stomach and nerves are so bad. I wondered if Mrs. Rigolo was mean natured like Pete's wife, but I never heard nothing bad about her.

Is what he said true? Are you going into the army? Annabelle says.

Yes, I told her.

Well, you know my boy is in the army, don't you?

No, I didn't know that.

Signal Corps, Annabelle says, as if that should make me remember.

But I guess I must still look kind of blank, because she says, You mean to tell me you didn't know Ralph?

I tried to think of Ralph who, because I didn't know Annabelle's last name, although I had seen her a lot and knew her first name.

Ralph Stegmeyer, you know.

He must have been a grade ahead of me, I said.

I will give you his name and address, Annabelle said, and if you should just happen to run into him, you can say hello.

She wrote down his name and address on a piece of paper and gave it to me.

After all, you can never tell, she said. Coincidences happen. Ralph has already run into his cousin from Indianapolis in the army. And it was by pure coincidence.

I told her all right, and walked out of the store with Penny's present.

Rigolo had walked out ahead of me and I saw him go over to his '62 Dodge and get in. Mrs. Rigolo was in there with him, so I guess there was nobody out watching the junk yard.

While I was walking to my Chevy, which I had to park over in the bank parking lot (which they let you do because it is too big for their customers and they say they want to have friends), I ran into Penny's older sister, Charlotte.

Hanger, she said.

I said what.

Hanger, I was just out to the Dairy Freeze and Phyllis wants to see you. She says it is urgent.

All right, I told her.

Penny will be home next Sunday, she said.

I told her I knew it.

Well I'll be seeing you, Charlotte said.

I told her good-by and then went to my Chevy and got in. I figured the make-up kit would be a coming home present for Penny, who would probably feel different about me when she got home, than the way she felt when she was talking to Judy Wechsler, the way Jim Boynton told me.

I went right back to the station and everything was real busy until almost ten o'clock, when Pete said, Somebody pulled the plug, and there was only this '64 Dodge pickup, which Bo was filling with gas. Pete was reading the newspaper with his feet up on his desk. Dean Fetz was back in the garage, spitting on his finger and rubbing it over an inner tube to find a pinhole leak.

I went across the street to the Dairy Freeze, which was a little bit crowded, but there was two high school girls helping Phyllis, along with Mr. Balakis, who owns the Dairy Freeze, and is almost seventy years old, but very wiry and small, with gray hair.

When I come up to the window, Phyllis says, Clyde Stout, I have been wanting to talk with you.

I know it, I said. Bo told me and so did Charlotte.

Phyllis whipped her apron off and said, Meet me around in back.

But I ask her if I could have a chocolate milk shake first, and she said yes and got me one.

I went around back and Phyllis came out the door and we were standing by the garbage cans. I ask her what it is she wants.

You don't want to drink your milk shake right here by the garbage cans, do you? she told me, so we walked down to the end of the lot where her Ford was parked.

Let's get inside, Phyllis said, so I can sit down and rest my feet.

Phyllis is a little bit heavy, as I think I mentioned, and she has varicose veins from standing in the Dairy Freeze all day. Mother says she sits when she is home and don't do nothing else. Her husband, Phil, does not mind, because he is lazy and doesn't care about nothing. Like the day I help him with Phyllis' dining room suit. He is always depressed, even when he is not in the Veterans Hospital with a nervous breakdown, and can't even hold a job. I always thought it was funny to have a man and woman married named Phil and Phyllis. Mother said people use to call her Phil until she got married and they had to stop so that they wouldn't confuse it with her husband's name.

Clyde, Phyllis said, I am worried about your mother.

I talked to her the other night, I said. Remember?

I remember, Phyllis told me. But one talk is not enough. Not only that, she hadn't gotten the letter when you talked to her last.

What letter? I ask Phyllis.

Phyllis sighed like she thought I was too dumb for words.

The letter saying you are drafted.

I was going to tell her the reason I had not understood was that Mother hadn't gotten that letter, I had. But I didn't say anything to her.

She is terribly, terribly upset, Phyllis said. And I think you should help her.

What can I do? I ask her.

Well, for one thing, you can talk to her.

I don't know what to say to her.

Clyde, your mother thinks the sun rises and sets on Clyde Stout.

That made me feel kind of funny so I didn't say anything.

You never realize what influence you have over her, Phyllis said.

Saying that seemed to give her an idea and she got excited all of a sudden. And other people too, Clyde Stout. One thing I have learned in this life, and I am almost as old as your mother, remember.

I told her I remembered.

One thing I have learned, Clyde, is that nobody knows exactly how much influence he has. What kind of an example he is setting, not only for younger people, like children, but for people the same age and even older people.

I didn't know what she was talking about so I started fiddling with the cigarette lighter on the dashboard, wondering if it worked. Only I was still listening, because Phyllis has a wonderful heart and she is always thinking of other people and how to help them.

She slapped my hand that was on the cigarette lighter, and the lighter popped out right after that.

Will you listen to me, please? she said, and I told her I would.

You are the Rock of Gibraltar to your mother, because it is just like she doesn't have a husband. At least he is never home, and don't you see that she has to depend on you as the man of the house? Can't you see that it is time you grew up a little bit and realized that you are a man now and must accept the responsibility of a man? Don't you?

Yes, I told her.

Well, why don't you then? You don't have to work so much of the time now that you will be going into the army before long. Spend some time with your mother and talk things over with her, help her plan her life for the time after you will be gone in the army, be a better pal for your little brother and sister.

I punched the cigarette lighter again, and she slapped my hand and said, Please leave that thing alone and listen to me.

I told her I would, and the cigarette lighter popped out because it was still hot.

You have no idea, Phyllis said, how important you are to other people. There are just a lot of things you have to learn.

She stopped talking for a little bit and just sat there nodding her head like she was agreeing with what she had just said.

Clyde, you walk around like you think you are just a

nobody. Sometimes I just get furious the way that Bo Thompson kids you, not to mention Pete. You don't have to take kidding from Pete just because he is your boss. Do you know that?

I nodded my head, and she pinched my arm and said, Do you?

I told her yes, I did.

Well, it is about time you act like it. If I were you, I certainly wouldn't let them call me that ridiculous name, either. Hanger. Clyde, you have to have more pride. You have to wake up. And I hope you don't start dating that Penny Barker when she comes back, because do you know something, Clyde? She just uses you. And laughs at you behind your back.

Two cars pulled out, filled with kids. They acted like they were going to drag, but they would get picked up if they tried that in town.

Phyllis surprised me and started crying a little bit then, and kept telling me to wake up because people could be rotten if you let them. And she didn't want to see a nice boy like me get hurt any more than was possible.

She sat there behind the steering wheel, sniffling and holding her hankie to her nose. I felt funny, and before I thought what I was doing, I reached for the cigarette lighter again, and she slapped my hand. But she didn't say anything. Her hand was a little bit wet from the tears.

Two cars came in then and took the two places left empty by the two cars that had just pulled out. Phyllis said she had to get back to work but she was awful glad she had had a chance to talk to me, because if a person did not have friends in this world, she said, what did they have?

20

I WAS thinking about Mr. Comisky and his nervous breakdowns and for a while wondering if I should even bother to go to his house to meet the four minute champion from Detroit. I had never heard nobody talk about the sport of free hanging, and I didn't mention it around, especially to Pete and Bo. Even though as I mentioned I was hanging out in the open now, except when there were customers or there was work to do. Pete and Bo didn't tease me any more when I was hanging than when I wasn't. It didn't seem to make much difference to them whether I hung or not. Because after that first day when Mr. Comisky give me the five dollars for hanging two minutes, that was all Pete and Bo needed for riding me and calling me Hanger.

On Friday I got a big envelope through the mail from Millford and it had some photocopies of newspaper clippings in it, all about free hanging as a new sport and endurance test.

The articles said it was already becoming a big sport some places and there was quite a lot of money bet on it and it was looked into whenever a town or state found out about it, which they didn't often do. Because not many people had even heard of free hanging.

One of the pictures showed a guy named Bert Wilderman from Detroit, who had hung four minutes and thirteen seconds. Mr. Wilderman's picture was circled with blue ink and somebody had written there, beside his head, This is your boy, Clyde.

I look at those pictures a long time and began to get kind of excited about hanging against this Mr. Wilderman. I only wish Mr. Comisky had told me about the thirteen seconds. All he said was four minutes.

He had called me on the telephone the day before and then is when I told him I had just barely made four minutes the day before that.

On the grease rack? he ask me, and I said yes.

I think we have the Detroit fellow beat, he says, with his voice calm, because you will do better in competition.

But I am not so sure, because I don't know how much difference it is going to make hanging from a bar instead of a grease rack. Also the Detroit four minute man will be in competition with me, just like I am with him. I don't know where there is a bar I can hang from, even to practice on. Except maybe in the playground of the junior high school, where I don't want to hang because everybody can see me and they don't know about free hanging as a sport.

Friday night after work I wrap up the make-up kit in brown paper and tie a string around it. I put a note on it, saying, From Your Unknow Admirer, forgetting the n on the word Unknown, which is what I always do. I could have kicked myself for forgetting this, because by the time I remembered, I had already stuffed the package in the Barkers' mailbox so that Penny's mother will pick it up, and I don't want to go back so late at night and go up on their porch to pick up the package and write another note for it.

Back when I was in the ninth grade, Miss Kessel said that I had adenoids and I did not pronounce my final d's and sometimes n, and that is why I never spelled them either. I spell exactly the way I pronounce words, Miss Kessel said.

Miss Kessel had red hair and an artificial leg.

Maybe it wasn't too late to go and get my package back. I couldn't forget about it, because I knew that if Penny saw that mistake in the word Unknown she would about die. And I wondered why I had to make a mistake like that just when it was so important to me. And when Penny was so sensitive.

So about one o'clock in the morning I decide to take a chance and go up on the Barkers' front porch and lift that package out of their mailbox, unless somebody had already got it, like Charlotte or Mr. Barker or Mrs. Barker.

So I parked the car about half a block away from their house and the street was very quiet. It was pretty light under the street lamps, but under the big maple trees that line the street, there were big dark spots because the leaves are very thick on those trees, which are healthy.

I parked my Chevy and walked slow and very quiet up the street because there was not a sound, except for some big semi changing gears at the traffic light over on Main. There was a light on in the second story of the house next door. An old couple lives there and I don't know their name.

When I got up on their porch, it seemed to me every board squeaked under my foot and I was sweating and hoping some cop didn't come along and arrest me for prowling around after 1:00 A.M.

But he didn't. And the package was still there, so I took it and went back to my Chevy and then just drove around on the Colchester Pike, which is a little county road, for a while to relax because I had been nervous up on the Barker's porch. I have never been in trouble with the police before, but there is always a first time.

I wrote the note again, and then decided that I would not put any note on the package at all. Just the package itself, which I would get up early Sunday morning when it was just getting light and put on the porch so that Penny would find it. Maybe she wouldn't even think I done it. But I didn't care because in a couple weeks I would be in the army anyway.

21

WHEN I GOT to the station, Pete come up to me and said, Hanger, did you hear about Phyllis' husband?

I told him no, and Pete said, He killed himself last night. Took an overdose of sleeping pills, and when Phyllis woke up this morning, he was gone.

I was carrying the clippings on free hanging for Pete and Bo to look at when Pete told me the news about Phyllis' husband and right away I could feel my hand start sweating around the newspaper clippings. I looked over at the Dairy Freeze with all the pennants flapping in the breeze, and there was Mr. Balakis standing at the window Phyllis was always standing at. There wasn't any customers around.

It is hard to believe, isn't it? Pete said two or three times shaking his head. He opened a pack of Spearmint gum and put a piece in his mouth. Then he offered me one, which I took.

I told him I couldn't hardly believe it either. Then Pete told me all the details, which I couldn't remember even five minutes later because the shock was so much. I laid the clippings on free hanging down on Pete's desk and started running my hand through my hair.

What have we got here? Pete said, picking up one of the clippings.

Those are some things Mr. Comisky sent me about the sport of free hanging, I said.

Pete just said oh, and looked back out the window.

Where is Bo? I ask him, and he said Bo got sick when he heard about Phyllis' husband because he knew him a little bit, and he went home.

A '65 Ford Galaxie come in then, and I went out and filled it with regular. It was somebody from out of town and I didn't know him.

When I went back in, Pete started talking about Phyllis' husband, saying how much mental trouble he had for years and how everyone was expecting him to go off the deep end some day.

Only you are never really prepared for it when it happens, Pete said, and I told him that was true.

Later on, we got real busy and Pete called Bo's home and ask if he couldn't possibly come in to work, which he did. But he was quiet and didn't joke or even speak to anybody for a couple hours, which was not like Bo.

Every now and then, I would look over to the Dairy Freeze and they seemed to be very busy, and getting along okay, only I'll bet that is the hardest Mr. Balakis has work for years, although he is a very nice old guy. Even though he does tell dirty jokes, which Phyllis never listens to. Mr. Balakis tells them to Pete and Bo and me. Especially Bo, who laughs harder than anybody, if the joke is dirty. I laugh too, most of the time.

Mother called me about noon, and she was mad that she was just now finding out about Phyllis' husband.

You would think they'd have told me right away, she said. After all, she said, I was one of her best friends.

Somebody told Mother that Mrs. Wilson, who is Phyllis' next door neighbor, went to the hospital with her where they pronounced him dead.

I didn't say much because we were kind of busy and I was hoping Mother would hang up.

Then she ask me why I didn't call her when I found out.

You know what good friends Phyllis and I are, she said. She sounded like she was going to cry, and I told her to get hold of herself because I had to get back to work, and she ask me why I was always thinking of work.

Then I just yelled into the phone. Mother, I told her, I have got work to do. I thought you already knew about it.

And then, right away, before she had a chance to say a word, I contradicted myself. I said, No, I didn't even think of you at all when Pete told me.

She was very quiet at the other end of the line and finally she kind of whispered, That is an awful way for a boy to speak to his only mother. An awful way.

But I didn't care, and all I did was say good-by and hang up.

I didn't go over to the Dairy Freeze and eat dinner, so I called Chet's place and had them fix a hamburger and root beer to go. I got a root beer instead of a milk shake because Chet puts too much chocolate in them. I went and picked it up, then I drove out to Rigolo's junk yard and he wasn't there, but Mrs. Rigolo was. She saw me and just wave at me to go on up in the lot and look around, and enjoy myself, the way Rigolo does.

I went up in the lot and sat down on the hood of a '53

Olds, which had had the rear wheel gears taken out for a man from Purserville who had wrecked his.

It was very warm and the sun shone on the metal of the hood, but I didn't care because all I could think about was Phyllis' husband and Phyllis. And then I thought about Penny a while.

Later on I took Mother to the funeral home and then to the funeral. Phyllis put her arms around me and cried when she saw me, and Mother put her arms around Phyllis and cried with her. We rode two cars behind the hearse all the way out to the cemetery, which was very quiet. Phyllis' husband did not have many friends. The minister said some prayers and his hair blew in the breeze, which was hot and very dusty. Nobody had sunglasses on and they were all squinting. I could hear a bird singing in some bushes nearby, I didn't know what kind. But it made me think of Rigolo's again, because out at Rigolo's there are a lot of birds that nest underneath the old cars, and almost every time I go out there I can hear them sing, which is very nice.

22

I DECIDED to keep the book by Farad Karaji because I do not think Penny would have like it, and that is one reason I bought her the make-up kit from Annabelle down at Hillary's Drug Store. Maybe I would take the book into the army with me, but I didn't know.

I read another poem that night after Phyllis' husband's funeral, when Mother went over to Phyllis' house with some chicken and dumplings and an orange spice cake which Mother makes delicious. She says that is when they need food, not right after somebody dies. I was up in my room alone after taking a drive up to Purserville with Jim Boynton, who didn't have much to say. This was after I finished work at the station, and I bought the milk shakes.

I wasn't sleepy when I got home so I read this poem from a section that said, Farad Karaji Says,

Stars
The rapiers of night
Slip
More silent than the light
Into my sleeping heart
Even when I am
Not aware.
Who can know what all his
Mortalities are?
And when?

Then I thought about Phyllis' husband. I had not heard him speak over fifteen or twenty sentences, I was thinking, and right then I could not have remembered what any of them were.

All I remember was he had a red square face and tiny eyes. He always looked like he was sunburn and his skin was sore. His voice was very soft so that you could hardly hear it, like that time at the auction house. Maybe he had spoke more words than everybody thought, only half of them were not loud enough to hear.

I went to bed after reading Farad Karaji's poem and then writing in my diary, and then when I woke up the next day, I decided to sell my car to Dean Fetz, who was a pretty nice guy and I would give him a good deal.

So when Dean come in, I told him about it and Bo Thompson overheard us talking and he started hooting and laughing about what a dump heap my '56 Chevy was. He had recovered from the shock of Phyllis' husband's death by this time and was very loud and talkative, like usual.

But Dean just kept quiet and when we got off for lunch, I let him drive the car while I went over to the Dairy Freeze. Phyllis hadn't come back to work yet, Mr. Balakis said, so he told me a joke about a circus midget and the fat lady, which I laughed at and thought was pretty funny, I told him.

When Dean comes back I am just throwing my milk shake carton away and Pete is putting new plugs in a '64 Pontiac with mags on the wheels. Bo is standing right on top of me ready to start riding me again, but I don't care.

So Dean tells me he is interested but doesn't have no

money, and I explain to him that it will be all right with me if he wants to spread the payments out, that I am not in a hurry about the money. And Dean said it certainly is a fair price, no matter what Bo says.

Then we talked a little while, and Dean says, It sure will seem funny when you are gone into the army, Hanger.

Right then I notice that Bo gets quiet and I know that he is feeling bad. One reason I don't get mad at Bo is I know how sensitive he is. He cannot stand strain the way some people do. Just Dean saying it will be funny when I am not pumping gas any more there at the old station made Bo get quiet and he did not kid or say a word until about three o'clock, when Roger McCloud and Don Wagner come driving in to ask Bo and me if we want to go to the drag races Saturday. I told them maybe, but I didn't say anything else, because I was hoping I might hear from Penny before then and we could go to the movies.

Mr. Comisky called me that afternoon right after Roger McCloud and Don Wagner left. He sounded very tired and kept taking deep breaths on the phone. I wasn't sure what he wanted, but I waited and finally Mr. Comisky said there might be a free hanger from St. Louis there too, and possibly even one from Louisville, Kentucky.

I ask him what their best time was, but Mr. Comisky didn't answer me exactly. What he said was, Clyde, you can't never tell what a man has got until you try him out. You know what I mean? I don't care if a man can free hang twenty minutes, he is not good unless he can do it in competition, unless he can hang there listening to the guy next to him panting for breath and saying to himself, I have got to outlast that other guy. He ask me if I understood.

I told him yes.

Clyde, he says, I know you have the right stuff.

And I said I hope so.

Then Mr. Comisky said something about maybe there would be trouble, but he didn't say nothing more. But just hung up, after saying, Wednesday is D Day.

After his call I wondered if free hanging is illegal, but I didn't know why it would be. Maybe it was the gambling, I thought. When Mr. Comisky had said there might be trouble, I thought he meant the police, but it turn out I was wrong.

But right then I wasn't sure, and it was all a mystery.

Later on that evening, we were very busy. Dean Fetz forgot to fill a customer's tires when he ask him to and he came back and was very mad, telling Pete what a poor worker Dean was. Dean felt bad and got mad after the man left.

At closing time, Pete had a few accounts to work on, which he usually does because he does not want to get home too early to his wife as she is always complaining and nagging. Bo had left a few minutes early to drive uptown and see if he could find Roger McCloud, who was going to sell him some fender flaps with luminous paint on them.

So I decided I would do a little hanging before cutting off from work, and I ran the grease rack up. Dean Fetz was just getting in his car to leave, and the garage lights were out, only the light from Pete's office was bright enough so I could see.

I jump up and hang there for a while, and then I begin to feel kind of funny again, and I know I am going to have a vision.

This time, the garage got darker, and then it was like

everything turned upside down. I mean, for a while there I felt like I was standing on my hands instead of hanging from them, and if I let go I would swing around and go feet first down to the ceiling of the garage, and the big jack and the tools and the tire rack would all be stuck there against the floor, which would be the ceiling.

Only I didn't let go of course, and after a few seconds I was sure that things were upside down.

Then is when I saw this big white light in the far corner of the ceiling, which was like the floor now. At first I thought it was a big jukebox, but then I see it is a lighted casket and it has a body in it dressed in black clothes.

For a while I think it must be Phyllis' husband, but then I am not sure. It is only a man's body, I was thinking, but I am not sure which man it is. I thought it might be my father, who wasn't even dead, even though the man in the casket was dead, I could tell. Then maybe Pete or Mr. Balakis or Rigolo or Mr. Comisky or any older man I knew, although I did not think it was Chet because I have never see Chet without his sailor hat on and mustache.

Then it seem like the whole garage start whirling around and I drop back to the cement and almost fall down, I am so dizzy. But everything is normal, and I look up at the clock and unless I made a mistake, I have hung there five minutes and eleven seconds.

But I don't feel too good about it, because I tell myself that if I am going to have visions very often when I am free hanging, I will not do it no matter how much money I can get.

Just then Pete slams his account book shut and yells out, Are you about ready to call it a day, Hanger?

I told him that I was, and Pete turned out the light.

23

THE NEXT DAY Phyllis was back to the Dairy Freeze, working just like she always was. Mother told her she didn't know whether it was right or not for Phyllis to go back to work so soon, but Phyllis told her she had a living to make, and then Mother told her she knew how it was to have to pull your own load.

When I went across at lunchtime to get my milk shake, Phyllis said, Clyde, it is wonderful the way your mother stood by me. She help me in a dozen different ways and I can never thank her enough. Also her Momma called from out in the country and told me how sorry she was, and we had a nice talk.

I told her yes, and Phyllis stood there hugging herself while I drank my milk shake and ate my coney island. I did not want to go around to the shady side of the Freeze and leave her there with nobody to talk to, since Phyllis like to talk so much.

Are you looking forward to going into the army? she ask me, and I told her yes in a way because it would be something different.

I bet you will miss your friends, she said.

I told her I would.

And Pete is going to miss you working in the station,

she said. Then she ask me how that new boy, meaning Dean Fetz, was working out and I told her fine and that he was going to buy my Chevy.

She said that was fine, but I think she already knew it.

And then she reminded me of our conversation about a week ago when we had sat in her Ford after dark and I had play with the cigarette lighter.

You don't know how people depend on you, Phyllis said.

And I told her that was right.

Then she told me it gave her a warm feeling to see me at the funeral because my mother and me were the best friends she ever had, and I was kind of surprise at that because I had know we were good friends but not that good.

And she ask me to write to her when I got in the army and I said I would and got back to the station where there were two Corvettes waiting for gas at the same time, which does not happen very often. They had just drove in because I see Bo wiping his hand on a grease rag and going up to one, and Dean was coming up to the other one. Dean has a funny walk, because he is so tall, I guess.

Along about two o'clock, somebody pulled the plug, and right then the phone rang and it was Pete's wife, who talked to him about twenty minutes. Only two cars come in while he was on the phone—a new Olds and a '56 Chevy four door, not in as good condition as my Chevy was.

When Pete hung up, Bo and I were in the office and he said, You know, that woman has a sixth sense. She knows the exact minute I have a chance to sit down and rest, and she calls me on the phone.

Bo was sitting on the window shelf, smoking a cigarette and he kind of laugh when Pete said this, blowing smoke out of his nose.

Hanger, Pete said, turning around in his chair and looking at me real hard and serious, what would you do if you were me and had a wife like I got?

I thought a minute and look out the window at Dean Fetz, who is leaving. Pete has just given him the afternoon off, because business was light, and Dean wanted to go swimming.

Before I could think of an answer to Pete's question, Bo said, What are you asking Hanger for? Don't you think you should ask somebody who's smart?

I was going to tell Bo off right then, because even though he was only kidding, and he is very sensitive, sometimes he goes too far. But Pete beat me to it. He said, Like who, Bo? Like you?

He ask it real sarcastic, and Bo just snorted through his nose and flicked some cigarette ashes on the floor.

And you can clean up the goddam ashes off the goddam floor too, Pete told him. You could tell Pete was really mad, and he is usually pretty good natured, so I figured his wife had said something to put him in a bad mood.

Bo cussed a little bit, but not at Pete, and he said, What's got into you? meaning Pete, and Pete said, Never mind what's got into me, just clean up the ashes like I said. If I want a smart answer to a question, I'll ask Hanger, and if I want a smart ALECK answer, I'll ask you.

Bo started to push the ashes toward the wastebasket with his foot, but when he saw Pete was still watching him, he cussed a little bit more, but still not at Pete, and went and got the broom and dustpan from the storage room in back. He looked at me when he walk by, like everything was my fault, but it didn't bother me none.

Well, Hanger, Pete said to me, what would you do if you was me?

You mean, with your wife? I ask him, and Pete nodded with his eyes closed, and said, Yes, with my wife.

I don't know, I told him.

I don't either, Pete said, and then he stuck his thumb and finger in his eyes and started to rub them, like he was getting a headache.

I don't either, he said again.

Then Bo came back after putting the broom and dustpan away, and he said, Well, has Hanger solved everything?

Bo, I said to him, one of these days I am going to stomp your ass.

Jesus Christ, Bo said. Can't anybody around this place take any kidding?

Too much is too much, Pete said.

Hanger, Bo said to me, do you know something? You've changed.

I have not, I told him.

You just don't know when to stop, Pete told him, and I said that was true.

Bo just stood there and looked at Pete and me for a minute.

Then he walk outside toward the pumps, and a '64 Dodge come in at the same time, and Bo filled it with regular, looking like he was mad at the whole world, which I guess he was. But he always gets over things. One thing about Bo, he doesn't hold a grudge.

That was all Pete said about his wife, except a little later on, when he told Bo that if he had asked him, Bo would have given him a lot of b.s., but he knew that I would give him an honest answer.

When you talk, Pete said to Bo, you are only thinking of yourself. Do you know that?

That's not true, Bo told him.

Yes it is, and you know it, Pete said. All you think about is your own words. You are thinking about how smart everybody is going to think YOU are, instead of thinking about the problem.

I've had enough lecturing, Bo said.

Maybe it's just that you have never had enough, Pete told him. You ever think of that?

Bo turned to me and said, For Christ's sake, you two really like to gang up on a guy, don't you?

I didn't say anything to Bo, even though it was just Pete ganging up on him, because it did seem to me that Pete was being pretty hard on him. Anybody who knows Bo knows you can't take him serious.

Hanger isn't dumb at all, Pete said. He just keeps quiet, and most people just figure he's dumb because he's quiet, but it isn't necessarily so.

All right, all right, Bo said.

I'll tell you one thing, Pete said, Hanger has the makings of a first-rate mechanic. He knows cars, and nobody can say he doesn't.

All right, all right, Bo said. I give up.

I wonder when business will pick up, I said, trying to change the subject.

Pete took a deep breath and just kind of look at me, and for a second Bo almost laugh out loud. I could tell.

I just wanted to change the subject, I told them.

Pete said, yes, that wasn't a bad idea, come to think of it, and he walk out of the door and just then a new Continental come in, but neither Bo or me made a move toward it, and Pete took care of it. He shoved the nozzle in the tank and started wiping the windshield, not talking to the driver like he usually does, but just looking serious.

Boy, does HE have a burr up his ass, Bo said, and then he walk out into the garage before I answer him.

Later on, Bo took off for the Dairy Freeze, when I had a '61 Pontiac at the pumps, and Pete had a DeSoto up on the rack, draining the oil.

Then a new Ford comes in, and Pete ask me where Bo is, and I told him. Pete cusses him again for taking off like that, but a few minutes later, Bo comes back with milk shakes that he had bought for both of us, and Pete didn't say anything.

Neither did I, only I felt kind of bad about getting mad at Bo, because he doesn't ever mean what he says when he gets smart like that, and I should of remembered, only I didn't.

When he handed the milk shake to me, he said, Here is a milk shake for you, Clyde, and that was the only time I have ever wished Bo had called me Hanger.

When we close up that night, I got in my Chevy and drove over to Penny's street, because I had not even seen her once since she got back from camp. Jim Boynton told me he seen her. Also he had a date right away with his girl friend, Judy Wechsler, and when he ask her how Penny was, Judy said all right.

When I drove by her house, I saw a light on upstairs,

but that was all. It was Penny's bedroom, but her sister, Charlotte, also sleeps in that room, so I didn't know who was up there. The lights were turned out downstairs, so I guess everybody has gone to bed early, and I wonder if Penny guessed who bought the make-up kit for her.

Also I kind of wish I had signed my name on a note when I left the kit, because she might think somebody else left it for her.

I just drove around awhile after that, wondering what the army was going to be like, and then I thought about hanging for Mr. Comisky, which would be the next day. I was getting kind of excited about it, since there were going to be hangers from Louisville and St. Louis there, as well as the four minute man from Detroit.

I wondered if they had visions like I had.

Then I hope I would never have another one, like that casket lying up against the ceiling of the garage and the world turned upside down.

Mr. Comisky said I should get plenty of sleep the night before, and I figure that was a good idea, so I went home to bed and did not read any of the poems of Farad Karaji. I wrote a few lines in my diary though.

24

I DIDN'T know what to do the next morning, because it was too early to go to Millford, but Pete gave me the whole day off anyway. I drove by Penny's house two or three times, but it look like she was not awake yet. She always likes to sleep late.

So I drove out to Rigolo's to look around, even though the old Chevy is not going to belong to me much longer, which gives me a funny feeling sometimes, when I think about it.

I go up and sit on the hood of an old Hudson, which they don't make any more, and look around at all the cars which I practically know by heart. I am going to miss Rigolo's junk yard when I go in the army. I sat there in the sunshine, squinting my eyes because I forgot to bring my sunglasses, and I listen to the birds chirping in the long grass that grows around the cars. Far away I hear an airplane, but I cannot see it. And I can also hear Rigolo using his drill down at the shed. From where I sit, the drill does not sound much louder than some bees buzzing, and everything is very quiet and peaceful and smells like grass and the hot metal of old cars.

Finally I drive back to the station because there isn't anything else to do, since everybody is working and I am the only one who is not. Phyllis waved for me to come over to the Dairy Freeze when I pulled in to the lot, but I pretended not to notice.

Pete is in a bad mood, and Bo has stayed home with a stomach ache. Just Dean Fetz and Pete are handling the station, but they aren't falling behind or anything. Still, I ask Pete if he wants me to help out, and he practically snap my head off.

Get the hell out of my way and have some fun, he told me.

Then he started in grumbling about how I only had a few days of civilian life left, and here I was wasting it. Some people don't know how to have fun, he told me, and I said that was true.

Then I glanced up at the Dairy Freeze again, about five minutes later. I saw Phyllis' hand waving up and down, and I knew she was waving at me still, to come over. I wish they had been busy and then Phyllis would not of been able to keep her eye on me the way she did.

Anyway, I crossed the street and walk up to her window, and she said, Clyde, who is this man you are going to see today?

I ask her if she meant the four minute man from Detroit, and she act like she is mad and shakes her head no.

You know who I mean, she says. The man who is in charge of this crazy business.

Mr. Comisky, I told her.

When I said this, Phyllis just closed her eyes and nodded. Then she said, Wouldn't you know. Just wouldn't you know.

Know what? I said.

Know that it takes a crazy man to think up a crazy idea, she said. She was staring at me now as if she could shoot me if she had a gun handy.

You mean Mr. Comisky? I told her.

Yes, I mean Mr. Comisky, she said.

For a second I just stood there, and she didn't say anything, and I was about to turn around and head back to the station, because I didn't want to hear Phyllis get started.

Don't leave yet, she said. I've got something to tell you, Clyde Stout, and I want you to listen good.

All right, I said.

I know this Mr. Comisky, Phyllis said, closing her eyes again and nodding her head up and down. He and my husband Phil were in the same ward at the state hospital.

I just listened and didn't say anything, because I had heard about Mr. Comisky and his nervous breakdowns from Charlotte. But as I told Pete and Bo, that five dollars he gave me was real. And they couldn't say it wasn't.

Clyde, Phyllis said, I don't want you getting mixed up with that man.

All he's going to do is pay me money to hang, I told her.

But he's INSANE, she said.

When she said this, Mr. Balakis came out, wiping his hands on a towel, and he said, Hanger, you hear the one about the steeple jack and the secretary?

I told him I hadn't heard that one, and Phyllis closes her eyes again and takes a deep breath like she could have shot both Mr. Balakis and me if she had a gun. But she took off to the back of the Dairy Freeze, because she knew the joke would be dirty, which it was. Mr. Balakis and I both laughed pretty hard, only he laughed louder than I did.

When Mr. Balakis left, he was shaking his head and still laughing, and Phyllis come back and starts shaking her head too, only she wasn't laughing.

Clyde, if you go down to Millford today, you'll be sorry, she said.

I told her maybe so, but I had already told Mr. Comisky I was coming, so I was.

Then I ask Phyllis if she would make me a milk shake, which she did. But she didn't say anything to me. She just acted like she wanted to put poison in the milk shake. And as a matter of fact, it wasn't as thick as she usually makes them. She knows I like my milk shakes thick.

25

THE ROAD to Millford was kind of crooked and narrow. At least, the county road, route 115, was, and that is the one I took because it was really faster and not so much traffic.

I had been to Millford a lot of times, but I still didn't know where Mr. Comisky lived, so I followed the directions he gave me and pretty soon I was driving on this side road, just outside of town, until I came to a big gate in a wood fence. The gate and the fence were all stained dark brown, and above the gate was a white sign saying BROAD ACRES, R. J. Comisky, who was Mr. Comisky's father, only he was dead now.

I drove down this road about a half-mile until I came to a big house which was all stained wood like the fences. There was a man riding a lawn mower under some apple trees on the lawn. He was going around in big circles, and he didn't see me pull up in my Chevy.

I drove around in back and there was a big garage that could hold five cars. Four of the doors was closed, and in the other one I saw Mr. Comisky's Cadillac, which I had fixed the tire for that day.

I drove the Chevy up to the edge of the gravel and got out. There were a lot of birds singing and trees all around and a bunch of shrubs here and there cut into funny shapes, kind of like big bottles and jugs.

I walked to the back door and knocked, and then a maid came out and told me to step inside the porch, that Mr. Comisky was expecting me.

You are Mr. Stout? she ask me, and I said yes, and then followed her inside. She was kind of fat and reminded me a little of Phyllis.

The maid went in the house, and left me there on the screened porch.

Then I hear some woman yelling, I DON'T CARE WHAT HE SAID.

Then there was footsteps and the maid's voice saying something which I couldn't hear, and the other woman, who I had not seen yet, yelling, THAT'S WHAT HE'S ALWAYS SAYING.

Just then, this old woman with rouge on her face and white hair sticking out all over comes out on the porch.

What do you think you are doing here? she ask me, her cheeks trembling she is so mad.

I have come to see Mr. Comisky, I told her.

What's your name? she said.

Clyde Stout, I told her. She just look at me, like she couldn't believe she had heard right, and I did something very dumb, then. I told her some people called me Hanger. I don't know why I said that, but I did. Maybe it was because I was afraid the old lady would have a stroke or something, she was so mad, and I wanted to talk to get her mind off of what was bothering her.

But it was the wrong thing to say, because she just yelled out, HANGER. DID YOU SAY HANGER?

And I said I did, and she just toppled back in a big wicker chair that was there on the porch. When she sat down, her legs flew up in the air, and I was surprised. It wasn't very lady like, the way she sat down.

Just then Mr. Comisky comes out on the porch, and I am glad to see him. He is dressed in long shorts that come to his knees. His face is very sunburned, so that his eyelashes are white, and he is smoking a cigar.

Well, he told me, I see you have met my mother.

I told him I had.

We have met, the old lady said, but we haven't finished talking yet. Have we? she ask, looking me right in the eye. I shook my head no, because I didn't know what to say.

You leave him alone, Mother, Mr. Comisky said. He really look mad all of a sudden.

I thought you had given this crazy business up? she said.

It's not crazy, Mr. Comisky answered. They always think something is crazy when it's just getting started.

The old lady said a word then which really surprised me, and I won't repeat it. Then she twisted around so hard the wicker chair snapped and cracked, like it was going to explode, and she yelled out, Patricia, bring me a Bloody Mary.

You better not drink, Mr. Comisky said, looking at me. Not until the meet's over.

Is anybody else coming out here for this crazy business? the old lady ask me.

I was hoping Mr. Comisky would answer the question, even though she was looking right at me. But he just smoked away on his cigar, like he hadn't heard anybody ask anything.

Well, I finally said, I guess maybe the four minute man from Detroit is coming.

Then old Mrs. Comisky just said that word again, nothing else. She sounded a little bit like Bo, because that is the way he always talks. And Pete, and Jim Boynton, and most guys, but it was a surprise hearing a rich old lady talk like that.

She was sure a lot different from Momma.

Pretty soon the maid name Patricia come in with a glass of tomato juice on a tray, and the old lady snatch it off like it was trying to get away from her. She drank about one third of the glass, and Mr. Comisky says, You believe in getting an early start, don't you?

Old Mrs. Comisky let her breath out and said, I have to start early, because I never know what the day will bring.

Just then, a car drives past the screened in porch, and parks beside my Chevy. I didn't even notice what kind of car it was, only it looked like a pretty new one. I wasn't thinking of cars, just what was going on between Mr. Comisky and his mother, and I was wishing I had followed Phyllis' advice and never come. I was even wishing Mr. Comisky had never come into the station, and then I would not be called Hanger by everybody.

A man got out of this car, and when he come closer, I see that is is Mr. Herbert.

Hello, Leo, Mr. Comisky said.

And Mr. Herbert come on to the porch and said hello to all of us. Then Mr. Comisky had the maid bring out some more glasses of tomato juice for everybody, except me, because I had to hang before long.

Did he arrive all right? Mr. Comisky said.

Yes. He finally got here.

Is that the four minute man from Detroit? I ask them, and they both nodded.

Only the guys from Louisville and St. Louis aren't coming, Mr. Comisky said, flicking his ash off his cigar.

When he said that, old Mrs. Comisky just went HA, very loud, but at first the men didn't say anything.

Shut up, Mr. Comisky told her then, but she just drank some more of her tomato juice and then smiled, with tears in her eyes.

Well, Mr. Herbert said, some more bad news. I couldn't get any of the staff boys to say they'd come out and take pictures. They're all busy.

Mr. Comisky said goddammit, real fast and under his breath, and then Mrs. Comisky said that word again, which I will not write down, and everybody was quiet a few minutes while they drank their tomato juice. The birds were chirping in the trees beside the driveway, and just then the fellow on the lawn mower came riding around the house, making a lot of noise, because it is a big seventy horsepower unit he is riding. Four cylinders.

Right then, Mr. Comisky jumps up and runs out the door, yelling at the man, who turns around and drives the lawn mower the other way. Then Mr. Comisky comes back and they all have some more tomato juice, which the maid has brought in on a tray.

Are you going through with it anyway? Mr. Herbert ask Mr. Comisky, and Mr. Comisky said he was, that he was no quitter.

Then Mrs. Comisky says in a loud voice, I AM NOT GOING TO LET YOU.

Says who, Mr. Comisky said.

Me. Your mother. I will not let you go through this crazy business on my property. If you want to make a fool of yourself somewhere else, that is your business.

Try to stop me, Mr. Comisky said. Just go ahead and try it.

I FORBID YOU, SON, Mrs. Comisky yelled. She spilled some of her tomato juice, she yelled so loud.

Well, I'll do it anyway, Mr. Comisky said. All we are waiting for now is this guy from Detroit.

Then he turn to me and said, Clyde, how do you feel?

I told him fine.

Muscles loose?

I guess so, I said.

Good.

Then Mrs. Comisky said that word again, which must of been a favorite with her. She took a drink, and I heard the ice cubes hit her teeth, she drank so fast.

Leo, Mr. Comisky said, some people just can't understand.

Mr. Herbert didn't say anything, because he didn't want to cross Mrs. Comisky, I could tell. He just sipped at his tomato juice. I found out later he worked on the Millford *Daily Times,* and just helped out for Mr. Comisky now and then, on special projects, like Mr. Comisky's planning to make a sport out of free hanging.

So now Mr. Comisky talked about free hanging. He said that when you really got down to it, all sports were a little bit silly. Like broad jumping. Why would people want to stand around and see how far a man can jump? There is no more reason for them to do this than there is for them to stand around and watch how long a guy can hang.

Then Mr. Comisky said that he figured all sports began as something people use to do to stay alive. Like running, he said. Running was a sport because it was one thing cave men had to do to escape from animals or catch them.

The same with enemies. And the javelin throw, he said, and shot put and things like that.

So why not free hanging? He ask why it couldn't be that men had to hang from trees when they fell off a cliff, and the man who could hang until he got some help was the man that lived.

There are all kinds of excitement, Mr. Comisky said, in the sport of free hanging.

Then Mrs. Comisky said her favorite word again, and Mr. Herbert didn't say anything.

Later on, when Mr. Herbert and me were alone together, he told me that he didn't object to going along with the poor damn fool, meaning Mr. Comisky, in his crazy schemes, so long as he got plenty of his expensive booze to drink and could have an expense account.

But that was after the hanging, and I will have to tell about that, first.

A few minutes later, Bert Wilderman, the four minute man from Detroit drove up in a battered old '49 Plymouth. If we had seen a car like that in the station, we would of kicked sand over it, as Pete is always saying. So nobody would see it and get scared away.

26

WHEN WE come down behind the garage, Mr. Comisky started cussing and slam his cigar down on the ground, like he was trying to make it bounce.

What's the matter? Mr. Herbert ask him.

The old bitch had them cut down, Mr. Comisky said. And then I look and see where several four by fours have been sawed off right above the ground. They had been creosoted, only their tops were white where the fresh wood had just been sawed. Mr. Comisky had called it the hanging court.

Mr. Herbert looked nervous and said, Maybe we better call the whole thing off.

After I come here all the way from Detroit? Bert Wilderman ask in a loud voice.

We all turn around and look at him because he sounded so mad. He was gripping his hands real hard and fast and breathing heavy.

Now just calm down, Mr. Herbert said. He stuck a piece of chewing gum in his mouth and started chewing real fast and looking far away at the sky. I wish he had offered me a stick, because my mouth was feeling kind of dry too.

The BITCH, Mr. Comisky said. Then he started walking around in circles slapping his hands against his head and stomach and muttering. Bert Wilderman, the four minute man from Detroit, was still gripping his hands and Mr. Herbert was chewing gum and he kept looking at me, as if he was wondering what I was going to do.

Maybe we better call it all off, Mr. Herbert said again, because Mr. Comisky acted like he didn't hear him the first time.

If Daddy's will had been right, Mr. Comisky said, I would own this goddam place outright, and I would kick her off. Then Mr. Comisky light another cigar and he had tears in his eyes. I wonder if he was going to cry because I have never seen a man cry with a cigar.

Let's do some hanging, Bert Wilderman said snapping his fingers. I've got fifty bucks that says I can out hang this guy, any day.

I was surprise to hear that was all the money that was going to be bet, but I found out later that Bert Wilderman's backers backed out.

Why don't we just forget the whole thing, Mr. Herbert says, and he glanced at the house. I could tell he was nervous on account of Mr. Comisky's mother maybe calling the sheriff, like she said.

No, Mr. Comisky said, everybody just wait right here.

So he went up to the house, and a few minutes later he came walking back carrying a large thermos jug, and he was wearing a big straw hat, kind of like cowboys wear.

Follow me, he said, and all of us did.

We walked across about five acres of lawn and then climb a fence and went into some woods, and then Mr. Comisky stopped and said, How about that limb there, boys?

He was pointing at a long low limb, about two feet above our heads. It was pretty big around.

Bert Wilderman dusted his hands together and squinted at the limb. He look a little like Pete when he is listening for a knock in an engine.

You mean, Bert said, you want both of us to hang from the same limb?

Why not? Mr. Comisky says. Right, Leo?

Sure, Mr. Herbert told him.

Nope, Bert Wilderman said. Too thick.

Well, Mr. Comisky said, turning all around, there are plenty of trees to choose from.

Bert Wilderman closed his eyes and said, like he was reciting a poem, Rules of the game: no give in the bar; bar easily grasped by both hands; bar must have uniform diameter for all contestants. Period.

Mr. Comisky slam his hat down on the ground and yelled at him then, You can't have EVERYTHING. Right, Leo?

I suppose so, Mr. Herbert said. He had spit out his gum and was drinking from the thermos jug. He hadn't even ask Mr. Comisky if he could.

Do you want to hang or not? Mr. Comisky said then, in a voice so low it was practically a whisper.

Do you? he ask again, when Bert Wilderman didn't seem to hear.

I do, Bert said, and then we all started walking again and looking for a good limb.

Finally we found one and then another one a few trees away. Mr. Comisky said that Bert could have his pick, so he took a few practice swings and then picked the thinner one, because it was easy to grab.

All right with you, Clyde? Mr. Comisky said.

I told him it was, so Mr. Comisky said, Take your places.

Mr. Herbert was about fifty yards away with the thermos jug.

Come up here, Leo, and help me with the timing, Mr. Comisky yelled out, and Mr. Herbert said all right. It sounded like he was farther away than he was.

Bert Wilderman was closing his eyes and taking deep breaths and gripping his hands again.

GET TO YOUR MARKS, Mr. Comisky yelled.

I saw Bert Wilderman's lips moving, like he was praying.

GET SET.

The leaves were crunching from Mr. Herbert's footsteps, but Mr. Comisky looked at him, and Mr. Herbert stopped walking and looked at his watch.

JUMP.

Bert Wilderman and I both jumped up and grabbed the limbs, only I might have grabbed mine a little bit before he did.

And then we were hanging.

I could hear a blue jay chirping up in the tree next to me, and I wonder what would happen if a bird come down and started to fly around your face and maybe peck at your eyes. When I thought that, I wonder if maybe I was going to have another vision, and I sure hope not.

Keep your eyes on both of them and see they don't regrip, Mr. Comisky yell out to Mr. Herbert. And then he said, This is going to be a fair contest.

After a while, everything was quiet, and then I heard Mr. Comisky yell out, ONE MINUTE. It was loud enough to make somebody like Bo jump out of his skin, but I could tell Bert Wilderman probably didn't mind and neither did I. He had a high threshold of pain, too, and was not nervous like Bo.

I thought of Penny for a while, and then Mr. Comisky said, TWO MINUTES, AND BOTH CONTESTANTS GOING STRONG. RIGHT, LEO?

I didn't hear Mr. Herbert answer the question.

It was when we were going on three minutes that I heard the birds start singing louder. It was like somebody had turned up the knob on a radio playing bird songs. And then things got kind of dark, only not very. I wasn't scared, only I was hoping I would not have another vision.

THREE MINUTES, Mr. Comisky yelled out. KEEP WATCHING THEIR HANDS, LEO.

Yes, Mr. Herbert said. I could hardly hear his voice, even though he wasn't very far away.

I tried to think of Penny again, but it was hard trying to remember exactly what she look like. My shoulders were really beginning to hurt now, and I remember what Mr. Comisky said, that the shoulders were never meant to put up with the strain of free hanging.

And then I remembered the poem of Farad Karaji. I remember all of it, because I have got a pretty good memory, sometimes.

Stars
The rapiers of night
Slip
More silent than the light
Into my sleeping heart
Even when I am
Not aware.

Who can know what all his
Mortalities are?
And when?

FOUR MINUTES, Mr. Comisky said. LEO, THIS IS A FOUR MINUTE HANG. I KNEW IT WOULD BE.

Mr. Herbert yelled out, Yippee. It sounded like he was under water someplace, only there was no water around.

It was then I started hearing Bert Wilderman breathing hard. He was pretty far away, but I could hear him breathing anyway. Just like he was right next to me.

FOUR MINUTES AND FIFTEEN SECONDS, Mr. Comisky yelled.

Then things got a little bit darker and I couldn't hear Bert Wilderman breathing any more, and all of a sudden I couldn't see anything except this old Hudson from Rigolo's junk yard. It had been wrecked pretty bad and was painted kind of a dull gray. Only now the whole car glowed like it was silver, and kind of furry, only even the fur on the car was silver too. And then there was pale green ripples going out from the car, like it had just splashed in something I could not see, except for these green ripples.

Right then, Mr. Comisky said, FOUR MINUTES AND THIRTY SECONDS, LEO. RIGHT?

I didn't hear what Mr. Herbert said, because right then Bert Wilderman shouted, LOOK OUT FOR THE GODDAM HORSES.

Then I didn't hear no more for a while because my arms began to hurt worse than I ever had anything hurt in my whole life. The nearest thing to it was a toothache I had once, only now it was all up and down both arms. My hands look like they was about ten feet away, and the birds were all quiet. Which they had been for some time, only I had not noticed.

Then Mr. Comisky said in a very calm voice that it was five minutes, and I still kept on hanging.

Finally I let go and drop to the ground because I could not hang any longer if my life depended on it. I figured Bert Wilderman had won the match, because nobody had said anything.

But when I drop to the ground, I look over at Bert Wilderman's tree and see him lying flat on the ground like he is dead or something. Except he is breathing real fast.

I kept seeing horses, I heard him say. But he wouldn't open his eyes.

Mr. Comisky come up to me then and said, Clyde, you are the winner and I want to congratulate you.

Mr. Herbert was just kind of standing there like he didn't hear. I figure he was too drunk to say anything.

27

AFTER THAT we went up to the house, where there was a big patio with yellow beach umbrellas over the tables. The tables were made out of iron and painted white. So were the chairs.

A lot of people started coming in for a cocktail party, and before long Mr. Comisky's mother come out too. She was all dressed up and wearing a lot of jewels and she was smoking a cigarette in a cigarette holder and talking very loud. She and Mr. Comisky didn't seem to be mad at each other any more.

Everybody was drinking, and I had a glass of ice tea and watch the man on the lawn mower. He was about a hundred and fifty yards away, making big circles around some flower beds. He kept it up until Mr. Comisky told a waiter in a white jacket to go and tell the man on the mower to go somewhere else. Which he did right away.

I notice a real tall woman with a big mouth and a turban on her head. She was kind of skinny, and she had a scar down one cheek. She had the loudest voice of anyone there. She called Mr. Comisky, Com, and she was always talking to him. I figured she was his girl friend.

After awhile, they all acted pretty drunk, and it was getting pretty late in the afternoon, and it was almost evening. Bert Wilderman had gone away, and Mr. Herbert was sitting in the shade beside the doors to the house. He looked sleepy and tired.

Then this tall woman yelled out, OH, COM, HOW CAMPY!

She said this several times, and kept laughing so loud, everybody else turned around and look at her, only she didn't notice, just flick ashes off her cigarettes, which she is always smoking.

I listened for a little bit, and found out that Mr. Comisky is telling her about the hanging contest. He is laughing too. I also remember that this tall woman has been turning around to look at me every now and then.

Finally she yelled out, Hey, Hanger, come over here and tell me all about it.

I went over, but I didn't say anything.

Then she ask if she could see my knuckles, and Mr. Comisky is laughing, but he did not look at me. His face is very red.

Then somebody turns on a record player and everybody starts to dance.

I went inside, and Mr. Comisky's mother is asleep on the davenport. She was lying on her back and snoring, and one shoe was off.

I walked around awhile, thinking that I might see Mr. Herbert and he could tell me when Mr. Comisky is going to pay me for the hang. But Mr. Herbert is nowhere around, and when I went back on the patio, there are more people there, but Mr. Comisky is not there, and nobody knows where he is.

The tall woman sees me after awhile, and she said, Hanger, if you are looking for Com, forget it.

Doesn't anybody know where he is? I ask her.

And she said, Nobody.

So I told her I might as well head back home, and she said that was a pretty good idea.

Then I went out and got in my Chevy and drove home.

28

THAT EVENING it started to rain, and the left windshield wiper on my Chevy flew off, which surprise me, and I drove a lot of the way home with my head out the window.

When I come in the house, Mother said, Well, what happened to you? Have you been sticking your head in a bucket of water?

I told her no, and then explained about the windshield wiper. It had stop raining by then and was very dark outside, even though it was only suppertime.

Well, she said, looking at me kind of disgusted.

Well what? I ask her.

Clyde, she said, you will be the death of me yet. Honestly, I have never known anybody who can aggravate a person the way you can. You know what I want to know.

About the contest? I ask her, and she said, Yes, about the contest.

So I told her what happened that afternoon, and when I finish, she is very mad. She closed her eyes and reach inside the neck of her dress and yanked very hard on something.

Well, she said, I certainly do hope this cures you of that silly hanging business.

I am going into the army anyway, I told her.

And that's the one thing I have to be thankful for, she said. Even though I don't want you to go, since you are practically my oldest child, but at least it will get you away from the likes of that man.

You mean Mr. Comisky? I told her, and she closed her eyes again and said, Yes, I mean Mr. Comisky. She sounded just like Phyllis when she said that. I certainly did get on both of their nerves, but I didn't care too much. I have always affected some people this way, but that is just the way I am. Especially when they are sensitive.

Anyway, Mother said that I would never see my money. She was sure that Mr. Comisky was a crook, and she told me so.

After awhile, I got tired of hearing her talking so much, so I went out and got into the Chevy and drove to the station. I figure that Pete and Bo and Dean Fetz would have to hear about the hanging contest sometime, and I might as well get it over with.

They weren't very busy when I drove up, and I was kind of sorry to see that, because now they would have more time to razz me. Even though I had won the contest from Bert Wilderman. It was still kind of dark out, and it look like it was going to storm again, so I guess people were not out driving around in their cars.

I didn't even look at the Dairy Freeze, because I saw when I drove up that there weren't any cars there, and I knew Phyllis would be having a fit trying to wave me on over to find out how the hanging went.

When I told Pete and Bo and Dean about the contest, they all whooped like a bunch of crazy Indians. Bo fell down on the floor like he could not stand up, his legs were so weak from laughing. Pete laugh till his face got red as a tomato, and even Dean Fetz laugh pretty hard. I didn't say much after I told them.

After a little bit, a '66 Fairlane comes in, belonging to a man named Holzaple, who is a good golfer and has an aunt who is drunk all the time and really makes a mess out of herself around the town, writing bad checks and things like that. She lives at Mr. Holzaple's house sometimes.

Anyway, Dean Fetz went out to fill the Fairlane with regular, because Bo was still lying on the floor where he fell down when he was laughing, and Pete was wiping his glasses off with a Kleenex. His eyes were watering from laughing so hard.

Hanger, he told me, they threw away the mold when they made you.

I didn't bother to answer him. Instead, I went over to see Phyllis, and of course she ask me all about the contest, and I told her. She said that was certainly too bad, and I would never see my money, and I told her probably not.

Then she didn't say anything for a minute or two, but just stood there kind of playing with her hair and looking out at the traffic going past.

Pretty soon I ask her, How's come you said you weren't surprised?

She just look at me and smiled, but she didn't answer, so I started to turn away, but she saw what I was doing, and she said, Clyde, do you really want to know?

I told her I did, but she didn't have to tell me if she didn't want to. But I said I was surprised that she wasn't surprised I had not collected any money, even though I had won.

You'll probably laugh if I tell you, Phyllis said. But you can't dispute facts, can you?

I told her you couldn't.

And the fact was, I wasn't surprised. And if you really want to know why, it's because I read your horoscope.

Do you mean the stars again? I ask her. She is always talking about the stars.

Yes, she told me, that's exactly what I mean.

And the stars told you I wouldn't get the money from Mr. Comisky?

Not in so many words. But basically, that is what they said.

He still might pay me, I told her, but she just closed her eyes and shook her head no. And then she started talking about houses and influences and the zodiac. I didn't know what she was talking about for a while, and then it seem like she was thinking I had lost the contest with the champion from Detroit, and I interrupted her, which surprised her a lot.

I didn't lose the contest, I said. I won.

But she just started in talking again, anyway, until two women came up and Phyllis told me to wait while she fixed them banana splits.

When she finished, the two women went over to a '65 Dodge convertible and got in and started eating their banana splits, and Phyllis started right in talking about my horoscope again.

Finally, she ran down, and I started to walk away, and she called out, Clyde, don't you want a milk shake?

I just shook my head no, because I was disgusted with everything and everybody. I knew afterwards that Phyllis would worry about me not drinking a milk shake, because she knows how I like to drink them, especially when they are thick.

Sometimes I wonder if she ever thinks of anything else.

That night it rained again, and there was thunder and lightning, so loud it woke me up, which it doesn't usually do because I am a sound sleeper. Once the thunder cracked so loud, I got out of bed and went to the window to look out. Then it crack again, right when there was lightning, so I knew it was very close. I saw the Chevy when the lightning lit everything up. There was water streaming all over it, but it was all right where it was parked in the drive, and Mother's car was in the garage. I was thinking that Dean Fetz was getting a pretty good car for the money.

Then I went back to bed, and when I got up, the morning was sunny and cool, and there was a nice breeze. I went downstairs and had breakfast. Mother tried to get me to drink two cups of coffee, because she said I would be drinking a lot of coffee in the army, and I told her that was true. Only I didn't finish my second cup because I didn't want it.

Then Mother said, Clyde, tomorrow is the big day, isn't it?

I said it sure was, and I was afraid that she was going to cry, but she didn't. She meant that tomorrow I was going in to the army.

How do you want to spend your last day at home? she ask me.

Oh, I don't know, I said.

Do you think you will go out to Rigolo's? she ask me.

I told her I probably would. Also I was thinking I would drive past Penny's house in case I would see her.

After breakfast I went out to the station, and I hung around awhile. I kind of wanted to go to work, but I could tell Pete didn't want me to. One time there was this MG come in to the outside pump and I started to go on out and fill it up, but Pete saw me and said, Hanger, leave that car alone. Then he yelled out for Dean Fetz to get it. He said Dean was lazy, but I think he was just grumbling. Bo was emptying the oil pan on a '64 Buick.

I watch him awhile, and then Pete told me to get the hell out of there and have a good time, so I went over to the Dairy Freeze, even though I would of liked to stay there and work. Phyllis was busy, but she said hello to me, and then I went back to my Chevy and drove out to Rigolo's.

It was a fine day, and Rigolo was in his shed reading a magazine. He said, Tomorrow's the big day. Right, Hanger?

I told him it was.

Then I walked up in the lot and looked at the cars. There were only four new ones in the lot, and two of those were wrecks we had brought in to the station. Pete had hauled both of them. They were both down at the far end, where Rigolo puts his new junk.

I knew all the other cars by heart. So I went up and down the rows, and I look at them. The birds were chirping and flying all around. I saw a sparrow fly right through an old Packard. The glass was all out of the windows. It was a '36, I think Rigolo told me one time when I ask him.

There were a lot of grasshoppers too, and they kept jumping up against my pant legs and falling off. I could smell the grass and the hot smell of the metal. It was very nice. I stayed there almost an hour. Then I come back and pat my old Chevy on the roof before I get in.

Rigolo come up and said, You selling your Chevy to Dean Fetz?

I told him I was.

Then Rigolo shakes my hand and says, Lots of good luck, and I drove away.

I drove by Penny's house a couple times, but she wasn't there. Then later on, Jim Boynton drives up beside me when I am waiting for the stop light at Carpenter Street and Bigelow to change.

Hey, Hanger, he yelled out, where you going?

I told him nowhere, so he tells me to follow him and we go to Chet's place and have a hamburger and root beer. Jim told me all about the drag races he went to on Sunday and I didn't say anything. I didn't tell him how the contest had turned out, and he didn't ask me.

That night I went to the movies with Jim Boynton. It was a cowboy picture, and it was pretty good. When it was over, I told Jim I better get home right away, because Mother said she wanted me there the last night before I go in the army, and she was taking it pretty hard about me going. She figure it was an awful thing to happen to her.

Jim said that was okay, and he would come home with me. Which he did, and when we got there, they were waiting with a big surprise going away party. There was Roger McCloud and Pete and Bo Thompson and Dean Fetz and Phyllis and a whole bunch of other people. Dad had sent me a telegram too, because he couldn't get away. He was in Los Angeles. He said he would visit me in camp, and I knew he would.

A couple years before, Dad and I had put up lights in the back yard. There was one on the garage and one on back of the house right over the patio and one at the back end, right below a big birdhouse we had on top of a twelve foot four by four, which I had given two coats of white.

The lights were all on and Mother had a big tub on the patio filled with cracked ice and root beer and 7-Up and Cokes. She knew I like root beer, and so did Roger McCloud.

Phyllis had brought her niece, who I had met once before at the Spring Festival out next to the hospital. She was kind of pretty, but she didn't talk much and neither did I.

Dean Fetz was asking me about the time I had rebuilt the transmission on my Chevy, and I was telling him. Right then Phyllis come up behind, only I didn't see her. She bumped my arm and made me spill root beer on my hand.

Where's the music? Phyllis ask me, and I said I didn't know.

Don't you have a record player?

Yes, I told her. There is one in the house.

But before I can go and get it, Phyllis ask me if I would write her a letter when I got in the army, and when I told her I would, she said, I'll bet.

Pete had brought his wife, who was sitting down in a lawn chair looking mad and chewing on the inside of her cheek and not talking to anybody. Right then Pete come up to Phyllis and me and said, Here's a toast to good old Hanger.

Then everybody kind of laugh and drank a toast.

Phyllis reached her arm around me and give me a big hug and said, Clyde, if I was twenty years younger, you would have to watch your step.

Everybody laughed again and then somebody had put a record on, and Jim Boynton and Judy Wechsler started dancing. Then Phyllis got Roger McCloud to dance with her niece and she swung around and made me dance with her. My hand was still sticky where she had made me spill my root beer on it, but she grabbed it anyway and made me put it around her.

We dance for a while. Phyllis especially like the real fast ones and she jumped around with a whole lot of energy. She was certainly having a good time.

After while she went over and talk to Pete's wife for a while. Pete's wife had said she didn't feel very good, and I heard Phyllis ask her what was wrong, but Pete's wife acted like she didn't want to tell her. Bo Thompson come up to me then and ask me how I think I will like the army. It was kind of funny, because it was like Bo and I hardly knew each other. He was acting real polite and he didn't try to kid me or anything. Neither did Pete.

Bo was telling me about his cousin who was in the navy, and Phyllis come up behind me and pinched me on the arm, and ask me why I didn't dance with her niece. I didn't say anything, and Phyllis come back two or three times and kept pinching me and telling me to go ahead and dance with her niece. But I didn't.

One time when she pinched me, Phyllis told me to forget about Penny Barker, and I said yes.

Then Mother told me Momma was on the phone, and she had called to say good-by and good luck. I talked with her about ten minutes and asked how the antique business was holding up and she said pretty good.

A little bit after one o'clock everybody started going home. Most of them had to get up early to go to work the next morning. And I had to leave early for army camp. All of the girls and women kissed me on the cheek, except Phyllis, who kissed me on the mouth, and her niece who shook hands with me. Phyllis cried, and said, Clyde, you have a lot ahead of you, and I told her that was true.

When Dean Fetz left, I gave him the keys to the Chevy, and he said he would take real good care of it. The army had given me a train ticket, and Mother was going to take me to the station the next morning.

I was tired and I went right to bed without reading any more of the poems of Farad Karaji. I didn't write in my diary, either. The next day Mother got up before daylight and drove me to the train and cried a little bit when she kissed me good-by. I was still sleepy. Then I got on the train and went to the army.

I figure I would write a letter to Penny from Basic Training, but I haven't gotten around to it yet. I have sent a funny post card to Pete and Bo and Dean at the station.

Sometimes I miss those guys and all the horsing around, and sometimes I think of Rigolo's. Mr. Comisky has not sent me any money, however, and I haven't heard a word from him.